ISLAND SECRET

Island Secret

MILDRED LAWRENCE

Illustrated by Paul Galdone

HARCOURT, BRACE AND COMPANY, NEW YORK

37717

Contents

ISLAND SECRET

To the Island

CHAPTER ONE

Bonnie sat on the box which held Mama's homemade quilts and stared straight ahead as the little ferry butted its way through the waters of Lake Erie. Fair Island was there, looking just the way Pop had always told her—rocks close along the shore, vineyards and peach orchards farther back, and rooftops sticking up through the greenery like rabbits peeping out of their holes.

"And the rooftop at the farthest tip of the island is ours," Pop had said over and over again, "even if it has to wait a while for us to come. Nobody but Bishops ever lived in that house, and we won't be the ones to change it."

Bonnie felt a little quiver of excitement, in spite of the way they were coming to the island—without Pop.

"But he'll come," she told herself stubbornly. "He said he'd be back, and he will be. And he'll know where to find us."

She glanced at Mama, leaning like a drooping flower on the rail. Bonnie was sure that Mama had given up hope of ever seeing Pop again, since the freighter *Nancy Belle* had come home to Boston without him. One of the other seamen, red-faced and unhappy, had brought Pop's sea chest with all his things in it around to Mama.

"He went ashore in Hong Kong, ma'am," he had said, twisting his cap around and around in his fingers, "same as the rest of us. And then he just never came back."

4

Mama had shut the parlor door then, but Bonnie had listened at the keyhole, a thing which Pop always said was sneaky, although in this case he might not have minded. Even then, all Bonnie had been able to hear were scattered phrases—"keep in touch with the boat company," "strange things happen in them far-off places," and "fine fellow, ma'am"—before the seaman, still twisting his cap, had handed Mama a leather purse full of money from the crew and had tiptoed ponderously out.

"Like a cat walking on flypaper," Pop would have said, with a special look for Bonnie. "Can't I get delayed somewhere without all this commotion?"

The commotion was still going on, and Bonnie hoped that it was the right kind of commotion, especially since this part of it was her own idea. Maybe after all it was going to be too hard for Mama to settle her family on Fair Island, which was where she had met Pop in the first place. Maybe Tommy and Cora Jane, the younger children, would not be happy here, either; they had certainly been most unwilling to leave their friends in Boston. Maybe—

Bonnie felt a small smile coming in spite of her worries. She could almost hear Pop saying, "Cut your suit to fit your cloth. It's hard to get a swallowtail coat out of a yard and a half of material."

The Bishops were lucky to get any coat at all out of their material, which was practically invisible now, what with the expense of coming to the island. Still, the sailors' purse remained safe in Mama's pocketbook, and here, at least,

5

they would have a free roof over their heads, vegetables from the garden Bonnie was planning to plant, and likely some odd jobs to be done for the summer people. In Boston, the rent would soon have eaten up every cent, besides everything else being high in proportion.

Ahead, Bonnie could see the dock coming nearer. She rounded up Cora Jane and Tommy, who were playing hide-and-seek on the deck. Cora Jane was seven, Tommy was nine, and Bonnie was going on twelve, but most days lately she felt twice as old as she really was.

"Such a responsible child," people had said in Boston when Bonnie had begun planning for the whole family while Mama wilted under her problems.

"Bossy," the landlady had declared angrily when Bonnie had demanded the three dollars that they had not used up on the rent when they left.

That was neither here nor there right now. The truth was that Mama was so dazed ever since the bad news about Pop that she didn't seem to take hold of things and so Bonnie had to do it. It was not exactly fun, but it was better than being walked over by people like the cross landlady.

"You got somebody meeting you to carry all this stuff off?" a roustabout inquired, eying the stack of boxes and valises.

Mama looked confused and then apologetic.

"I thought—" she began.

"We paid freight on everything," said Bonnie firmly. "That means you deliver it—on the dock."

6

"Big for your size, ain't you?" the roustabout grumbled.

"I'm big enough to read, anyway," Bonnie retorted. "It says right on the ticket—"

"All right, all right. We deliver it—on the dock. Seems you're young to start haggling already."

Bonnie tossed her black braids defiantly, but she could feel the tears coming to her eyes. Pop never liked what he called "bossy females" either, but it seemed somebody was always ready to take advantage of people who did not stand up for their rights. Bonnie's job right now was to get the family to Fair Island safe and sound and with a few dollars left over, no matter who liked it or who didn't.

She looked again to make sure the island had not disappeared. Pop always said it was so beautiful that it might vanish into thin air like something magic, and Bonnie could understand what he meant. The boat was close enough now so that she could see the haze of faraway pink which would be peach trees in blossom and a cluster of dots which would be the school and the church and the general store if none of them had burned down in the years since Pop had seen the place. She turned her head a little farther, saving the best for the last, but at the far tip of the island she could see nothing but tall waving treetops and, on a rocky knoll at the water's edge, an indistinct mass of gray.

"The old winery," she told Cora Jane and Tommy. "You remember Pop telling about it."

"Pop said it was nothing but a rheumatic bruin any more," said Tommy.

"Romantic ruin," said Bonnie, who was used to Tommy's rather uncertain vocabulary. "Whatever it is, it's going to be exciting."

The winery had been there time out of mind, Pop always said, even before the Bishops had added the little piece of land where it stood to their own property. The winery itself had been abandoned years before Pop was born and had been a play place for two generations of Bishop children. Bonnie was not quite sure how it was going to look, although Pop had tried hard enough to tell her. She had a vague notion of gray stone walls, layers of dusky cellars hung with cobwebs, and imaginary pirates lurking in the shadows.

Even the Bishop house, she supposed, would be full of cobwebs, for it had been almost four years since Great-Uncle Eben had died and Pop had inherited the place. Pop had never had the time or money to come back, but one of the neighbors had spread sheets over the furniture, locked the door, and mailed Pop the key.

"A roof over our heads," Pop often said, balancing the key on his palm. "You never know when you might need one."

You never did, Bonnie agreed as the ferry blew its whistle and edged up to the dock. She glanced at her mother, who had tears in her eyes.

"You get off the boat with Mama," Bonnie told Tommy and Cora Jane. "I'll wait and see that our stuff gets unloaded all right."

There was not very much, considering it was everything they owned—a barrel of dishes, boxes with linen and bedding, a brassbound trunk, and three shabby valises. It would have been too expensive to bring the furniture, even if Mama had not needed the money it brought to pay their fares. Bonnie counted every piece as it left the boat and as it arrived on the dock. She did wish that one of the boxes might have held her tortoiseshell cat, Arabella, who had had to be left behind in Boston with the next-door neighbors. Pop always liked Arabella because she reminded him of the Bishops' island cats, who had all been marked with black masks over their faces like raccoons.

"The robber barons, we used to call them," he often told Bonnie. "All gone now, I expect, even with nine lives apiece. A man forgets how time passes."

Bonnie comforted herself with the thought that Arabella had a good home, but even that did not quite erase the little lonesome feeling of having no cat to sit, purring, on the doorstep.

"We're here," she said in a voice which she tried to make as cheerful as possible. "Now all we have to do—"

"There used to be a man with a horse and wagon down to meet all the boats," said Mama unexpectedly.

"And there he is," cried Tommy, who had already been exploring the dock. "Right over there."

The man stepped up, tipped his hat and said, "Alexander Pippett, ma'am. Would you wish your things taken somewhere?"

9

"Oh, yes," said Mama in a relieved voice. "If you would."

"Been here mighty close to twenty years for just that purpose. Now then, where would you be going?"

"The Bishop place," said Mama anxiously. "Do you know where it is?"

Mr. Pippett nodded.

"That place has been here longer than any of us. If you'd wish to sit on the wagon seat with me, the children can hang their feet over the tailgate, and you can all go right along with your things. No extra charge, naturally."

Bonnie, who already had her mouth open to ask the price in advance, closed it again. One look at Mr. Pippett's rosy face with its fluff of white mustache and its bright blue eyes told her that he would not be one to take advantage.

With all three children helping, everything was loaded into the wagon, which was drawn by two dignified white horses.

"These folks are going down to the point," Mr. Pippett remarked to his team in a conversational tone.

The horses pricked up their ears, looked at each other, and obediently turned down the shore road.

"They understand every word I say," said Mr. Pippett proudly. "If they want to, that is."

"What are their names?" asked Bonnie from her perch at the back of the wagon.

"Albert and Almira. Named 'em for some cousins of

mine, on account of there being sort of a resemblance in the face." He turned to Mama. "You'd be Edith Johnson that was, I expect. Your folks were summer people, as I recollect."

"Not really summer people," said Mama in a voice which told Bonnie that she was pleased to be remembered. "My folks came from Cleveland every year to run the dining room at the Summit House. Just while the resorters were here."

She smiled wistfully, and Bonnie knew she was thinking a long time back to when she had first met Pop.

"Your husband's still following the sea, I'll warrant," said Mr. Pippett. "He's a mighty fine fellow, like all the Bishops. There's nothing beats a good island boy, to my way of thinking."

A tear spilled over onto Mama's cheek, and Bonnie hurriedly said, "Pop's been delayed. He—he was in China the last we heard."

"Well, you couldn't find a nicer place to wait for him than right here," said Mr. Pippett cheerfully. "The point's a sightly spot, in spite of—" He seemed to change his mind about something he had been about to say. "You'll find the house some run down, being vacant and all." He pointed with his whip. "Speaking of which, we're practically there."

Ahead of them, on the shore side of the road, an untidy tangle of shrubbery bulged from behind a rusty iron fence, which seemed to be trying in vain to hold the mass inside. Under a tall oak festooned with trailing vines, a weather-

beaten house sprawled in ells and wings as though unde-
cided exactly where to go. The iron gate sagged open to
show the faint traces of a brick walk leading to the front
porch.

"Needs a mite of work done on it," said Mr. Pippett.
"Nothing that can't be fixed." He wound the reins around
the whipsocket and prepared to climb down. "We can
bring your things in this way the easiest. You got your
key, ma'am?"

Mama wordlessly produced the key.

"Let me!" cried Bonnie in excitement.

With Tommy and Cora Jane close behind her, she scurried up the sagging steps, fitted the key into the lock, and
pushed open the door.

"Phew! Dust!"

Bonnie hurried to send the dark-green shades flying to
the tops of the windows. Sunshine streamed in on dust
which eddied across the floor, made fluff-balls under the
sheeted chairs and tables, and floated in the air like mist.
Cobwebs hung from the ceiling, and a pair of startled
spiders skittered across the floor. Mama picked her way
up the steps, lifting her skirts gingerly at sight of the dust
in the parlor.

"You sit down, Mama." Bonnie carefully lifted the pro-
tecting sheet from a horsehair chair. "I'll—I'll help Mr.
Pippett."

What she really wanted to do was to dash off behind
Tommy and Cora Jane on an exploring tour, but that

would have to wait. She did stop to open the folding doors into the big dining room and to put up the shades there, too, so that everything would look more cheerful—if dust really did look more cheerful mixed with sunshine.

She gave a little start as a twig cracked just outside the bay window and something shadowy disappeared around the corner of the house. All of a sudden, the sunshine did not seem as bright as it had nor the island as friendly as Pop's stories had always made it out to be. Unexpectedly Bonnie longed for the familiar sounds of Boston—wagons rattling over the streets, the fish peddler crying his wares, even the explosive motors of the new-fangled automobiles.

"Tommy! Cora Jane!" called Bonnie. "Come help Mr. Pippett with the boxes."

The sound of her own voice was some comfort, and she could take time later to worry about strange noises and moving shadows. Mr. Pippett had brought in the first box and was standing in the middle of the parlor.

"As I recollect," he said in a puzzled voice, "there used to be a walnut desk right in that corner."

"The desk with the secret drawer, maybe," cried Bonnie. "Pop told me about it lots of times. He used to keep his coin collection in the secret drawer, so his sisters couldn't get at it—and his money from trapping muskrats, too."

Mr. Pippett looked more puzzled than ever.

"Maybe it's in one of the bedrooms, though I never knew Eben Bishop to move things around much. Well, you can look into that later. Right now we better get the

13

rest of your things inside. There's a cloud over yonder that looks like rain."

While Tommy went outside to help Mr. Pippett unload the wagon, Bonnie found an old broom in the kitchen and swept out a place to put Mama's barrel of dishes.

"We'll just use the dishes right out of the barrel until we can scrub the cupboards," Bonnie told Mama, who had spread out one of the sheets and was kneeling on the floor to unpack the first boxes. "Tommy says there's stovewood in the shed, so we can start a fire and heat some water right away. Mama, it's going to be all right. It's—"

A harsh voice interrupted her as a tall figure appeared at the back door.

"You folks got any right here? Trespassers ain't even allowed on the premises, much less inside the house."

Bonnie looked up at a hulking man in dirty, patched overalls and a battered straw hat, which he did not bother to remove. "Squinch-eyed," Pop would have said, and not the right kind of squinch-eyed, either. Sailors got squinch-eyed from looking at the sea and the sun all day long, but this man looked as though he was squinch-eyed from pure meanness, likely from scowling most of the time. Bonnie stepped up to him, ready to do battle.

"Certainly we've got a right here!" she said. "We own this place. And if trespassers aren't allowed, that means you, too!"

"Got a deed or anything to prove it?" the man de-

14

manded. "Anybody can say they own property—ain't no sign they do."

"It's a sign we do!" Bonnie could feel her temper slipping. "We've got a deed, right there in Mama's pocketbook, but I don't know any reason why I should show it to you."

The man backed away a little.

"Man can't be too careful who he believes. Never saw you folks before in my life."

"You see us now," said Bonnie. "We're Luther Bishop's family, moving into our own house."

"Where's Luther then? Left you high and dry, I've no doubt! He always was a one to go gallivanting all over."

Mama, looking like an indignant kitten, got up from beside the barrel of dishes and stood beside Bonnie.

"My husband followed his trade, which was the sea," she said in a quivering voice. "He was always—"

"Now, now, what's all this?" Mr. Pippett, followed by Tommy, came in with the last two valises. "Homer Hinchley, I'd hate to think you've been deviling the Bishops—and them just getting settled, too."

"Friendly advice never hurts," said Hinchley with a grimace which barely passed for a smile. "They'd be making a big mistake to stay here. House run down, place all grown up to weeds, cold winters, no way for a woman and a passel of kids to make a living. I'd hate to see it, I surely would."

15

"You'd do well to look the other way then," said Bonnie, "because we're staying."

Mama laid a cautioning hand on Bonnie's arm.

"Be a little gentler spoken," she whispered. "A lady never argues with strangers."

Cora Jane, dusty and disheveled, came clattering down from upstairs.

"I couldn't find that desk anywhere," she announced. "Not in all four bedrooms or in any of the closets or even in the attic."

Mr. Pippett looked thoughtfully at Homer Hinchley.

"Seems you might recollect something about that desk," he said. "It was a walnut one—sat in the corner there. Saw it myself the day of Eben's funeral."

"It had a s—" Bonnie began, but Mr. Pippett looked hard at her and talked a little louder.

"You might ask around some," he told Hinchley. "It's possible somebody might have—uh—borrowed it and would want to bring it back, now the folks've come."

"How would I know?" Hinchley blustered. "I live on the next place, sure, but Eben Bishop and me never neighbored none, not after that trouble we had over the boundary line. And I still say—"

"Everybody knows where that line is," said Mr. Pippett, "and I'll take pains to show the folks here, so's they won't get over on your side and maybe wear out the weeds." He looked hard at Hinchley. "G'by, Homer. You watch out for that desk."

Hinchley shambled toward the door, turning for a parting shot.

"You kids better stay away from that old winery of yours. Snakes in them rocks, floors liable to fall in, being so old and all—"

"And an earthquake due any year now," said Mr. Pippett tartly. "As I said, g'by, Homer."

Bonnie stared after Hinchley's retreating figure. Tomorrow, first chance she got, she would explore the winery. A little shiver ran up her back at the thought of what she might find. Snakes? Falling floors? And what else?

Explorers

CHAPTER TWO

I F THERE's anything that takes your mind off your worries, it's having twice too many things to do," Pop always said.

Bonnie felt sure that this was true as she climbed out of bed the next morning with her mind full of a dozen things that ought to be done that very instant, not counting a hundred more for later on. Dust to be brushed away, floors to be scrubbed, mattresses to be aired, weeds and grass to be cut in the yard—Bonnie counted everything over in her mind and decided that something was going to have to wait for another time. Certainly nobody was going to be out of work for days and days, not until the garden was put in, some of the window screens patched, and the porch steps fixed where they sagged at one corner.

All these chores seemed like nothing as Bonnie leaned from her bedroom window into bright May sunshine. An apple tree had burst into scented bloom during the night, and Bonnie smiled at a robin who was singing at the top of his lungs among the pink-and-white blossoms.

From her little room just off the kitchen, Bonnie could hear Mama's soft footsteps and the plop-plop of cornmeal mush boiling on top of the stove. Mama was humming a little tune under her breath, as she always did when she was cooking for her family. She did the same thing when she was sewing, too, which was often, for Mama made everything for the children and for herself, from ruffled petticoats to the low-necked embroidered pinafores which Cora Jane wore over her lace-edged batiste blouses. Bonnie wished that she could feel as Mama did about sewing, but Bonnie was all thumbs when she got a needle in her hand and was apt to feel more like crying than singing.

Bonnie hurried out to make sure that there was plenty of wood to keep the stove going for the gallons of hot water which Mama would need to scrub the clothes and the children after the long trip. The rusty pump outside the kitchen door worked, for a wonder, as Bonnie had already discovered.

"Good deep well, too," Mr. Pippett had said the day before. "Safe for drinking, and it's never gone dry in fifty years that I know of. Now, if you need any help, feel free to call. My house is right on the other side of that pasture." He smiled at Bonnie. "All you have to do is let out a good loud holler and my cow, Cleopatra, will moo—being a woman, she can't stand for anybody else to get a word in edgewise—and I'll hear her and come right on over."

Pumping more water for Mama, Bonnie hoped that they would need Mr. Pippett for something very soon, because she was anxious to see whether Cleopatra really would relay the message as Mr. Pippett had said. In any case, having Mr. Pippett on one side balanced having that horrid Homer Hinchley on the other.

Bonnie sighed. It seemed she could not possibly wait another minute to see where everything was on their own place and up and down the road. Instead, she ladled hot water from the stove reservoir into the dishpan and handed Cora Jane a dish towel. Mama had already started to take down the lace curtains in the parlor.

"So dirty they'd stand alone," she remarked cheerfully. "Tommy found some curtain stretchers in the attic, so I can do them up as easy as not. We'll wipe down the walls and then air all our sheets and quilts if we can find enough bushes to lay them on. They smell musty even being packed such a little while."

Bonnie was glad that Mama had lots of cleaning up to do because it would keep part of her mind off the fact that Pop was not here. Mama did love to wash things. In fact, Bonnie thought that Mama sometimes liked things better than she did people because things never said or did anything to make her feel shy or self-conscious.

"Your mama," Pop used to say teasingly, "scares easy. She doesn't know that a lady as pretty as she is can have everything her own way if she'll just say what she wants."

Mama always blushed whenever Pop talked like that, and she kept on being just as shy as ever—and just as pretty, with her wide blue eyes and her flyaway blonde hair that never wanted to stay neatly in place. Bonnie's never wanted to stay put, either, but when hers got loose from its tight braids it merely straggled, while Mama's curled up into little ringlets, much prettier than her usual sedate coil.

"I wish we had some fresh milk," said Mama. "You children can't just drink water. Do you think—"

Bonnie immediately thought of Mr. Pippett's cow, right in the next pasture. Bonnie had dreams of their having a cow of their own sometime, but meanwhile she would ask Mr. Pippett if they could buy milk and cream from him. Mama could even make butter in the old wooden churn which was sitting in a corner of the kitchen.

Finding such ordinary things in the house as the churn and the stove and the old rush-bottomed chairs had already made Bonnie feel much less as though she were walking into something strange and possibly dangerous. The clock on the mantel, ticking wheezily since Bonnie had oiled it with a feather, and even the rusty old pump seemed to bid her welcome as one of the Bishops come home at last.

"I found a little china kitten on my dresser," said Cora Jane, "and a hat with an ostrich feather on my closet shelf."

"We'll find lots of wonderful things when we have time to look," said Bonnie. "Oh, I can hardly wait. The attic and the barn and the winery and—and everything."

Bonnie had already stuck her head into every room in the house but not long enough to take in all the details. A long leisurely look would be just like an Easter egg hunt —something exciting in every corner.

It was the middle of the afternoon before Mama, who had been busily ironing clothes, pushed the irons to the back of the stove and sat down in the rocker.

"I'll have to make a list for the grocery store. All three of you better go, because I'll need sugar and flour and navy beans and—" She looked apologetically at Bonnie. "It's quite a long way."

"But think of all we'll see!" cried Bonnie. "We might even get acquainted with some of the neighbors."

"I don't want to get acquainted any more with that old Hinchley," said Tommy. "He's an awful billion."

"Villain," said Bonnie. "But think of Mr. Pippett. He's just as nice as Mr. Hinchley isn't."

Mama took some money out of her purse and handed it to Bonnie.

"Make it go as far as you can," she said.

Bonnie nodded.

"I'd better buy some vegetable seeds while I'm about it," she decided. "The sooner we get our garden in, the sooner we'll be eating off the land."

Naturally, Bonnie knew as well as Mama did that they could not grow everything they ate. She was planning to earn some cash for the other things by peddling vegetables to the summer people, who, Pop always said, were crazy to get home-grown produce.

"Hens," thought Bonnie. "I wish we had some hens."

Hens and a cow and garden seeds—it did seem that there were quite a few unexpected things a person needed to start out in a new place like the island. Bonnie shooed Tommy and Cora Jane down the road ahead of her, hurrying them along especially briskly past the mustard-yellow house which must belong to Homer Hinchley.

She hesitated at the next place beyond, a tall white house with a wide veranda all the way around and fancy scroll-work dripping from the eaves. The lawn was smooth and green and the round tulip beds were bright with color behind their low wire fences, but the shades were tightly drawn at all the windows.

"Summer people," said Bonnie. "Maybe a market for vegetables—and right close to home, too."

"Don't you set foot on that lawn!" Homer Hinchley's harsh voice made Bonnie jump. "Mr. Lewis wouldn't like it."

"I'm not setting foot on that lawn," said Bonnie. "The road's still free, I suppose, or are you keeping people off that, too?"

"Mr. Lewis don't like people gawping at his house. Get along with you, now!"

Bonnie stood her ground.

"You attending to this Mr. Lewis's business—whoever he is?" she demanded. "Same as you attended to ours, I suppose, without being asked."

"I'm Mr. Lewis's caretaker," said Hinchley triumphantly. "He's a big man from Chicago, if you must know. You paid your taxes?"

"What taxes?" asked Bonnie.

"Property taxes, of course. If you don't pay your taxes, your place gets sold, you get put out, and—"

"Of course we paid them!" cried Bonnie in vexation. "And Mama has the receipts, too—not that it's any of your business." She beckoned to Cora Jane and Tommy. "Come on, children. We've got better things to do than this."

"And don't be hanging around over here!" Mr. Hinchley called after her. "The Lewises will be here soon, and they don't like people—"

"—gawping at their house," Bonnie echoed. "I should think they'd be glad to have people gawping at it when they aren't there. If somebody had been gawping at ours at the right time, we might not have lost that walnut desk."

She took one look at Homer Hinchley's hanging jaw and hurried on down the road.

"I don't like that man," said Cora Jane, slipping her hand into Bonnie's.

"Who could?" Bonnie wondered. "Those Lewises must be strange people, to hire him for a caretaker."

Heading on down the road, Bonnie was glad that Mama had not been there to hear her talk the way she had to Mr. Hinchley. It was not that Bonnie did not know that you were supposed to say "Yes, sir" and "No, sir" to grown-ups. It was just that there was no use letting Hinchley get the idea he was going to have anything to say about how the Bishops did things.

From the road, Bonnie could see Mr. Pippett at the dock waiting for the ferry to arrive. The horses, Albert and Almira, were standing patiently, doubtless ready to go almost anywhere as soon as Mr. Pippett explained to them where it was. Bonnie waved enthusiastically and ran down to the dock.

"We're going to buy our groceries," she announced breathlessly. "We're getting settled just fine, and Mama found some curtain stretchers, and could you spare us— sell us, I mean—some milk?"

"Might work out a deal," said Mr. Pippett. "You know how to milk?"

"I could learn," said Bonnie, confident that she could do anything if she had to.

"Milking's a useful talent," said Mr. Pippett, "and Cleopatra'd be glad to see somebody's face besides mine. I'll bring you around some milk tonight, and after that we'll figure something out. You seen Hinchley today?"

"Down by the Lewises'. He wanted to know if we'd paid our taxes. What does he do for a living, with so much time left over to mix in other people's business?"

"A little of this and a little of that, like most of us island folks. He caretakes for the Lewises, if you can call it that, and he has some peaches and grapes down back of the house, and he does some fur buying. Buys up whatever pelts he can get around here, though most folks'd rather sell direct to dealers from the mainland—not so apt to get rooked. He buys furs in Canada, too, and traps some himself—makes a regular business of it."

27

Bonnie nodded. Pop had told her about trapping musk-rats in the winter in the marshes that edged part of the lake.

"You folks have some marsh of your own alongside Hinchley's before you get to deep water there by the winery," Mr. Pippett went on.

Bonnie was not much interested in marshes, which she thought were probably fuller of snakes than they were of muskrats.

"What's that big island over there?" she asked.

"That's on the Canadian side. Rock Island. In the sum-mertime you can ride over there on the excursion boat."

All the way home with the groceries, Bonnie was silent and thoughtful, hearing hardly a word of Tommy's and Cora Jane's chatter. She had forgotten that Canada was right out there. It made her feel as though she had traveled a far distance—not really far the way Pop traveled but at least almost into a foreign country.

"Bonnie!" cried Cora Jane. "There's a hole in the bean sack."

Bonnie retraced her steps to gather up the beans.

"Let 'em go," said Tommy. "What's a few beans?"

"Takes money to buy 'em," Bonnie retorted, "and we can't spare a single one. There! I guess that's all."

She was tired when she got home, but with Mama's permission she set off to explore the winery, with Tommy and Cora Jane whooping happily around her.

"I found an old spyglass in my room," said Tommy.

"I'm going to pretend I'm a sailor like Pop, up on a pinnacle."

"It's a binnacle," said Bonnie. "And you don't go up on it. It's just a glassed-in box with a compass and a light in it."

Everybody, it seemed, had found fascinating things in the house except Bonnie, who had not had time to look. At least she was getting a chance to look at the winery, which probably would have nothing at all in it except fresh air.

The building was covered on the land side with ivy, which stirred like a green tapestry in the breeze and somehow, to Bonnie's mind, made the building seem warmer and more alive. Glassless windows stared at her, but she stepped eagerly over the threshold into a large room, from which, she knew, steps led down story by story into the two cellars.

"Down there's where Pop used to play," said Bonnie, peering down the stone steps leading to the dim depths below.

"What did he play?" asked Cora Jane.

"Hide-and-seek sometimes when the girl cousins were visiting," said Bonnie, "but mostly things like pirates or robbers."

Almost she could hear Pop's voice telling her all about it, describing everything so clearly that she could see in her mind how everybody looked—the fat cousin who got stuck hiding in an old wine barrel once, the prissy girl

29

cousin who was always afraid of getting her hair uncurled in the damp air, the big brother who made little wooden boats for them all to sail in the shallow water at the edge of the lake.

"Let's go down in the cellars," said Tommy, who remembered better than Cora Jane the stories which Pop had told. "I read in a book once where some people found buried treasure down in a cellar."

Bonnie tiptoed behind Tommy down the wide stone steps into another big room, which smelled of musty earth and old wooden barrels. A little light filtered down from upstairs and from a small window cut in the wall on the lake side. There were two cellars, one below the other, Pop had explained, both blasted out of the side of the rocky hillside so that their back walls were all natural underground rock. The built wall on the side toward the lake descended straight to the water's edge.

"People from the other islands used to bring grapes in to the winery by boat, I've heard," Pop had said. "There was a dock once, though it was gone long before my time."

Bonnie hesitated at the head of the steps leading to the second cellar. She was not quite sure whether she cared about being so far away from the sunshine. Still, she could not let Tommy and Cora Jane go alone.

It was darker in the second cellar, and the single window was very small and very dirty. A weathered door with a rusty hasp was probably the one through which the grapes had been unloaded from the lake in that faraway time.

Bonnie stumbled a little on the stone floor, which was uneven and layered with dirt.

"It's certainly dark," said Tommy. "I'm going to bring a lantern next time and pretend I'm an explorer in darkest Africa."

"I don't think that's the kind of 'dark' they mean," said Bonnie, "but a lantern's certainly a good idea."

A sudden rustle from the corner sent a shiver up her spine as she hurried back up the stone steps. If she had been alone, she would have run up two steps at a time and rushed outside, away from—

"A mouse," she told herself. "Nothing but a mouse."

She sighed with relief when they were all upstairs again in the big room with the sunshine pouring through the windows.

"You can see ten miles with this spyglass, I guess." Tommy struggled to pull out the extensions on the old brass telescope, which had not been out of his hand since he left the house. He steadied it on one of the wide window sills and squinted out over the lake. "I can't see a thing. It's all blurry."

"Just keep moving the extensions back and forth until it's right," said Bonnie. "Like this."

She picked up the spyglass and tried it. For her, everything was clear—the store and the church far down the shore to the left, Mr. Pippett's house to the right, the waves and the gulls and the whipped-cream clouds. Suddenly a boat seemed to jump practically into the telescope from out in the lake. Whoever was in the boat was holding something in his hands and looking very hard toward the wine cellar. Bonnie squinted her eyes to see better.

"Oh!" She set down the spyglass in disgust. "That Homer Hinchley! Everywhere we go, there he is, even in our telescope! And he was looking at the wine cellar with a pair of field glasses of his own!"

She simmered with annoyance all the way back to the house.

"Mama," said Tommy between mouthfuls of bread and milk at supper. "You know that old—"

Bonnie kicked him warningly on the shin.

"Ow!" said Tommy. "Bonnie kicked me."

"Excuse me." Bonnie fixed Tommy with a stern eye. "We had a lovely time today, didn't we, in spite of all the work? Everything was lots of fun."

Tommy nodded obediently.

"Lots of fun," he echoed.

"Mama'd just worry," Bonnie explained later when the children were doing the dishes.

"I guess so." Tommy rubbed his shin and looked pitiful. "I think I've got a confusion."

"Contusion," said Bonnie. "Here, have another cookie. Might make your leg feel better."

Turning in her bed that night, Bonnie wished that she could forget some of the unaccustomed country noises. A cool breeze blowing from the lake brought with it strange rustlings, the occasional raucous cry of a sea gull, and odd sounds that Bonnie could not even identify. Something thumped on the roof, and Mr. Pippett's Cleopatra mooed in her pasture.

Bonnie finally pulled the covers over her head and tried not to listen to any more noises. It did seem, though, that the birds might stop twittering so late at night and that whatever wild animals were crashing through the underbrush might better be at home in bed.

"Just mice and songbirds and maybe a rabbit," she told herself reassuringly.

An unusually heavy-footed rabbit seemed to be walking near the kitchen door. Something scraped against the house —could Cleopatra be out for a stroll with all the rest of the creatures?—and there was a rasping sound like a stick being drawn along a picket fence. Bonnie huddled closer under her covers and finally fell asleep.

She dreamed that Homer Hinchley was rowing a boat up the lane between the apple trees and yelling, "You can't live in that lighthouse! Mr. Lewis wouldn't like it!"

Crash! Thud! Thump! Hinchley's boat must have struck a rock. Bonnie sat bolt upright in bed. Out by the shed she could hear the heavy-footed rabbit again, perhaps even two of them, and both in a great hurry.

"It's n-nothing!" Bonnie quavered to herself, knowing all the time that the crash and the thud and the thump had been real. "N-nothing at all!"

Pigs

CHAPTER THREE

Bonnie awakened the next morning to still another
strange sound. In Boston she would have known what it
might be—a dog scratching on the door or a sparrow flying
against the window screen—but on Fair Island, so full of un-
familiar noises, she was afraid even to guess. She finally
stuck her head cautiously out from under the covers and
stared into a black-masked little face at the window. A tiger
cat had hooked its claws into the screen and was shaking it
as though trying to attract Bonnie's attention.

"One of Pop's robber barons! Wait! Oh, please wait!"
Bonnie leaped out of bed, streaked for the kitchen door
and held it open. "Here, kitty, kitty!"

The cat strolled inside in a dignified manner, inspected
Bonnie's bedroom carefully, jumped up on the window sill
and began to wash his face with a busy paw.

"Oh-h-h!" Bonnie sighed with pure pleasure. "I do hope
you'll stay." The cat looked at her and purred loudly.
"Your name can be Robbie—for robber baron."

When Pop came, he would be glad to see that one of the
descendants of the old Bishop cats was still here. In the
meantime, Bonnie was glad, too, not only because Robbie
would comfort her a little for having had to leave Arabella
in Boston but also because it was probably Robbie who had
been responsible for all the strange noises the night before.
At breakfast, she poured half of her milk out into a saucer

for her new pet, who already acted as though he owned the Bishop house and everybody in it.

"Like the lord of the banner," said Tommy.

"Manor," said Bonnie.

She intended to keep a sharp eye on Tommy, who was apt to vanish with a book into some secret hiding place of his own unless somebody caught him first.

"We're going over to Mr. Pippett's," she announced firmly. "We have some business to talk over."

"Me?" asked Tommy. "You mean me?"

"Certainly, you. Cora Jane can stay and help Mama."

Bonnie was tempted to yell and see if Mr. Pippett's cow would answer, but she decided against it. It would be better to save the yelling for something more important than just announcing that she was coming over.

Mr. Pippett was outside feeding his hens, all of whom he addressed cordially by name—Griselda, Fatima, Theodora, Katrinka, Hepzibah.

"Wish you'd do me a favor," he said. "See that lame hen over yonder? Name's Anastasia. It's considerable trouble feeding her separate so the others won't grab off all her food. Wish you'd take her home and look after her. Fact is, I'd give you a setting of eggs for your trouble. Setting on those eggs would be good for her—give her a little rest, you might say."

"Well, thank you. I'll be glad to."

"You can have the little chicks, too, whenever she hatches them out. Got more eggs around here already than

I can eat. Now, about this business of the cow. If one of you wants to milk for me, I'd be glad to spare all the milk you need. You could make me some fresh butter now and then, too. Not as young as I used to be—seems I can't do everything under the sun any more."

"Me!" cried Tommy. "I can milk. I read how in a book once."

Tommy looked so eager that Bonnie did not have the heart to tell him that she had been planning on doing the milking herself. Still, she was going to be busy enough helping Mama with the butter and taking care of Anastasia and, especially, planning ways to make some money.

"You'll be wanting to put in a garden, I guess," Mr. Pippett continued. "I'd take it as a favor if you'd let me bring Albert over to plow it up for you. He needs some extra exercise the worst way. Getting fat and worthless. Just bring me some fresh vegetables now and then if you want to."

"You think of everything," cried Bonnie. "I never knew anybody so kind-hearted."

Mr. Pippett looked embarrassed.

"One lick for you and two for myself," he said in an offhand voice. "If your mother'd bake me a pie or some bread once in a while, I'd be glad to pay her for her trouble. I'm not what you'd call a first-rate cook myself."

"She'll be glad to," said Bonnie. "Mama loves to cook."

"Thought so. Had a look in her eye. Now tell me all about your father."

Bonnie saw that Tommy was safely out in the pasture talking to Cleopatra, who chewed rhythmically and twitched an ear now and then as though she understood every word he was saying. Bonnie poured out the whole story of Pop's mysterious disappearance.

"Mama doesn't think he'll be back," she confided, "and neither do the sailors. But I do, Mr. Pippett. Whatever is keeping him, I think he'll get out of it. He—he said he'd be back."

"You keep right on thinking that way," said Mr. Pippett encouragingly. " 'Twon't do any harm, and it might do a world of good."

Walking back home with Anastasia tucked under her arm and a setting of eggs in a basket, Bonnie was glad that she had told Mr. Pippett all about Pop. She was not sure that Mr. Pippett thought Pop would be back, either, but at least he had admitted that there was a chance. Mr. Pippett was certainly a nice man with his talk about the Bishops doing him favors when all the time he was doing everything he could to help them.

Cora Jane burst out of the house to meet them.

"The desk!" she said. "The desk came back!" She danced ahead of Bonnie and Tommy. "Out in the woodshed when I went to get the kindling."

Mama came trailing out with her hands all floury.

"Bonnie, I just don't know what to think," she said in a worried voice. "How in the world could anybody bring it back and we never know it?"

"There were lots of funny noises last night," said Bonnie, "but I thought it was only Robbie."

She rushed out to the woodshed, with the whole family at her heels. The desk was there, thrust into a corner as though someone had intended the Bishops to think that it had been there the whole time.

"But it wasn't! You know it wasn't!" Bonnie looked thoughtfully at the desk. "Well, anyway, it's here now. Let's carry it into the parlor."

For Mama's sake, she tried to act very offhand about the whole thing, as though it were perfectly natural for somebody to bring back their desk in the middle of the night.

"I think it was Mr. Hinchley," said Tommy.

"Shhh!" said Bonnie. "So do I, only I don't know why he brought it back, unless he thought we might go to his house sometime and see it there."

"He probably wouldn't let us in if we did go," said Tommy.

"Of course not." Bonnie mimicked Homer Hinchley's harsh voice. "Mr. Lewis wouldn't like it."

The desk looked very handsome in the parlor, in spite of several scratches and a thick layer of dust.

"I'll have to wait until fall for some black walnuts," said Mama, "so I can rub the stain over those scratches. Right now I'll just wipe the whole thing with a damp cloth and rub some oil in. Dear me, it couldn't have been dusted the whole time it was gone."

Bonnie was busy opening all the drawers—three big ones

down below and several little ones up above. She found nothing but dust in any of them.

"There might be something in that secret drawer," she said, "only Pop never told me how to find it—said he never was one to tell a secret."

She went over the whole desk, pushing and pulling at every bit of carving she could find, but no secret drawer sprang out at her, and no hidden compartment opened to reveal Pop's old coin collection.

"Not that the coins would be there now, anyway," Bonnie decided sadly.

It would be exciting to find the secret drawer, even with nothing in it, and of course it would be twice as exciting if there actually was something inside—an old letter or a ribbon or anything at all.

"We'll just have to keep trying," said Bonnie, leaving Tommy and Cora Jane to go over the desk for the fourth time.

In the days that followed, hunting for the secret drawer became an automatic action with Bonnie. She would sit in the parlor in the evening, with Robbie curled at her feet and the lamp beside her and would run her hands over and over the desk, imagining that the wood gave a trifle here or bulged out a trifle there.

"Pop will tell us where it is," she insisted stoutly, "as soon as he comes."

It seemed to her that he was a long time coming, but at

least she was glad that the place was beginning to look more the way it must have when Pop had last seen it.

"As though people lived here, anyway," she told Mama.

The house was spotless inside, with stiffly starched lace curtains which Bonnie hoped would make people forget that fresh wallpaper was needed inside and fresh paint outside.

The yard was cut and raked, and the lilac bushes, freed from strangling vines and weeds, were thick with purple blossoms. The garden down by the marsh was plowed and planted, thanks to Mr. Pippett and his horse, Albert, and already curly pea shoots were pushing their way out of the black earth beside the pale green lettuce and the feathery carrot tops. Bonnie, with Tommy and Cora Jane as reluctant helpers, pounced on every weed as soon as it appeared.

"I don't like to weed," Tommy complained when Bonnie sent him down one morning to thin out the long rows of carrots. "What do we have to grow all this stuff for, anyway? We never did in Boston."

"We'll eat it this summer, and Mama's going to can a lot of it, and we'll sell some to the summer people for ready cash. And of course the potatoes and turnips and all that can go into the root cellar for winter. You scoot along now. I'll be down to help you pretty soon."

Bonnie was glad that the summer people were starting to arrive. Although she would never have said so to Mama, she was a little lonesome. All the children on the island were still going to school, so she never saw any of them except trudging past with their lunch buckets in their hands. Bonnie would have gone to school, too, except that she had hurried up and finished her grade in Boston before she left and there was no sense in doing it twice. She hoped that ringing doorbells at houses which were now closed and seeing new faces while she sold vegetables would make her feel less like a stranger on the island.

"Bonnie! Bonnie!" Tommy's voice came faintly from the garden. "Shoo now! Get on out of here! Bonnie! Come help me!"

Bonnie tossed her dish towel in the general direction of the kitchen table and rushed for the back door. A dark animal hurtled past her, and then a second, and then a third.

"Pigs!" cried Bonnie. "Horrid old pigs!"

Still another pig charged toward her. Bonnie dodged as it tried to rush between the house and the woodshed.

"Shoo!" yelled Bonnie. "Go home, wherever that is!"

She flapped her apron, and the pig veered through the open door of the woodshed. Bonnie slammed the door and fastened the hasp.

"Just stay there, until we see what this is all about," she cried.

She found Tommy looking in despair at the garden. The lettuce bed was practically all rooted up, a wide swath was gone from the carrot rows, and big craters marked the center of the potato field.

"Oh!" Bonnie stared angrily at the ruined garden. "All

that work gone, and just when we could have sold some things to the summer people. Now, whose—"

Tommy jerked a thumb toward the Hinchley place.

"His," he said. "He's the only one that raises pigs right around here."

Bonnie started for the fence.

"I'll tell him a thing or two!" she cried. "He just better keep his old pigs at home." Her gaze fell on a neatly cut hole in the fence. "Look at that, will you! That was cut on purpose. You can see where the metal's still shiny."

Tommy looked at her, round-eyed.

"What are you going to do? Should I go get Mama?"

"Mama went to the store, and anyway I can manage this myself, only I'll have to think a little. See if you can find an old piece of wire in the barn and we'll try to mend the fence. Then we'll rake up the field so we can plant some more seeds right away. Oh, that Hinchley! I could—"

She could almost hear Pop saying, "Simmer down a little, Bonnie. Being mad's like sitting in a rocking chair—fills the time but doesn't get you anywhere."

Bonnie leaned against a tree and thought for a long time. Just scolding Mr. Hinchley was not going to do a bit of good except to relieve Bonnie's mind, and nothing in the world would keep him from letting his pigs out again any time he took a notion. Suddenly Bonnie remembered something.

"Tommy!" she called. "Come with me. We're going to talk to Mr. Hinchley before we do anything else."

44

"He'll know he's been talked to when you get through with him, I betcha," said Tommy. "Don't you take any nip off of him."

"Lip," said Bonnie. "You just listen while I talk. Don't say a word, no matter what."

Hinchley, smirking disagreeably, met them as they came across his back yard.

"Neighboring back and forth already," he said in pretended amiability. "Everything all right? Garden stuff doing good? No bugs? No worms?"

"Everything's fine," said Bonnie sweetly. "We just came to see if your pigs got home all right. A lot of them were rooting up our garden, and it'd be a shame—"

"Can't keep pigs from getting out," Hinchley blustered. "Anyhow, how do you know they're my pigs? Pigs're pigs, seems as though—one about like another."

"You could be right," said Bonnie. "That one I've got locked up does look like every other pig I ever saw. Black with a white band around his middle. Well, finders keepers. Mama was just saying some nice fresh pork would taste good."

"Hey!" said Hinchley. "That sounds like one of my pigs. You can't go around butchering other folks's pigs. You can't—"

"Might be able to find something else for supper if our garden was to be replanted and the fence mended," said Bonnie blithely. "Either way—makes no difference to me."

"I'll get the constable," Hinchley yelled. "I'll have you arrested for having stolen property. I'll—"

"You said yourself they probably weren't your pigs," said Bonnie, "so maybe the constable would think they weren't, too. Well, good-by. We have to go now."

"You wouldn't dare," Hinchley bellowed after them.

Bonnie and Tommy kept on walking.

"We'd certainly like to have that garden all fixed up again by noontime," Bonnie called back, "and we wouldn't want any pigs getting in it again either. We're real good pig-catchers, day or night. Come on, Tommy. We have to get everything ready."

"You—you—" Hinchley was practically speechless.

Bonnie grinned at Tommy as they decorously turned in at their own front gate.

"You wouldn't really, would you?" asked Tommy.

Bonnie patted his shoulder soothingly.

"Keep calm now," she advised. "We have to do a little play-acting."

Bonnie and Tommy carried the grindstone out of the barn and set it up back of the woodshed where it would be sure to be in full view of Homer Hinchley. Not quite sure whether she had the right weapons, Bonnie brought out an ax and a long carving knife, which she sharpened on the grindstone while Tommy turned the handle. The grindstone made a loud rasping noise against the metal, and sparks flew from the turning stone.

"He can't help noticing that," said Bonnie. "Tommy, can you make a noise like a pig squealing?"

Tommy grinned and lifted his voice in a piercing squeal. "Squee-ee-ee! Squee-ee-ee!"

"You could hear that in the next county," said Bonnie in satisfaction. "Try it again."

"Squee-ee-ee! Squee-ee-ee!"

Homer Hinchley burst out of his house and rushed over to the fence.

"You killed him already?" he demanded.

"In a little while," said Bonnie. "We've about decided to sue you for damage money, too. That garden truck the pigs spoiled was nearly ready to sell to the resorters, and we have to earn a living some way."

Hinchley looked at her determined face.

"Wouldn't be too hasty if I was you," he said. "I'll fix up your garden. Just give me that pig back."

"You'll get him back as soon as the garden's fixed," said Bonnie. "If it's today, that is. And don't forget to mend the hole in the fence." She hesitated thoughtfully. "I wouldn't want to promise about not suing you, though. We could have gotten a good price for that produce."

Hinchley went off, muttering to himself, and in a few minutes the children could see him down in the garden, raking and hoeing furiously and presently patting in new seeds and patching the fence.

"You fooled him all right!" said Tommy.

"Took some figuring, though." Bonnie sat down on the

kitchen step and began to laugh. "The face on him! He looked as though he were going to explode like a firecracker."

She was still laughing when Hinchley came up to the house and sullenly demanded his pig.

"Think you're smart, don't you?" he grumbled.

"Me?" said Bonnie. "Smart? Oh, my, no! Why, how could I be smart? I'm not even grown up yet." She cautiously opened the woodshed door. "There he is. I expect he'll be glad to get home."

The pig catapulted through the doorway, tipping Hinchley into the rosebush beside the path, and headed for home. Hinchley picked himself up and examined a thorn scratch on one hand.

"I'll get even!" he vowed. "None of this woulda happened if—"

"If you hadn't turned your pigs into our garden to tear it up," said Bonnie placidly. "Good-by, Mr. Hinchley. Thank you for everything."

"You're a sight too sharp-tongued for your age," Hinchley muttered, stamping off toward home.

"He's mad, all right," said Tommy. "Bonnie, what's the matter? Aren't you glad you beat him down?"

Bonnie nodded. She was glad about that, but she was sorry that she had to be the kind of a person who could do it. What Hinchley had said about her being sharp-tongued was the truth, and the truth, as Pop and everybody else always said, was what hurt the most.

"I wonder what he'll think of next," said Tommy.

"Something disagreeable. We'll have to keep a close watch and ask Mr. Pippett to watch, too. Well, let's put all this stuff away." She shivered. "I even scared myself with all that talk about fresh pork for supper."

She walked slowly into the house. Now that a good half of the vegetables were ruined, she would have to think of some other way to earn money right away. Maybe she and Tommy could find some odd jobs to do for the summer visitors. Summer was about the only time to get jobs, anyway, because the island people mostly took care of their own work without any help from anybody. Tomorrow Bonnie would have to start asking around, to get her bid in before anybody else. She did wish she could think of something unusual that people might want done. Just asking for work probably would not get her anything. It would be so much better to say, "Do you need your elephant washed?" or "May I polish your gold tooth today?"

"Bonnie! Bonnie!"

Cora Jane, who had been at the store with Mama. rushed up the front walk, leaving the gate swinging behind her.

"Bonnie, the Lewises have come! Mr. Pippett was bringing them and their things when I came by. My, but they're elegant! Such clothes! There's a mama and a papa and a girl about as big as you. She waved to me, too. Bonnie, could we go right over and get acquainted?"

Light on the Subject

H ORRID OLD THINGS!" Bonnie slapped her hand against the screen door, and a squadron of fish flies flew sluggishly away. "Never saw so many bugs in all my life!"

She went outside with the broom, stepping over piles of dead fish flies in front of the windows, where the lamplight had drawn them to dash all evening against the glass. Bonnie sniffed the fishy odor which came from the dead insects. Considering how many died every day, it would seem that soon there would be no more left, but Mr. Pippett said they would keep coming for two or three weeks yet. They hung on the sides of the houses, flew up in clouds whenever anybody touched rosebushes or shrubbery, and collected in odorous heaps under the street lamp beside the general store.

"Canadian soldiers is their right name," Mr. Pippett had explained, "but around here we call them fish flies or June flies, one or the other. Whatever their name, we could do without them."

Bonnie thought so, too, as she swept the brick walk in front of her while more fish flies settled where she had swept the minute before. They clung thickly even to the neat sign which she had painted and set up on the fence—*Fine Sewing and Dressmaking. Baked Goods.* So far, Mama was not baking for anybody but Mr. Pippett or sewing for anybody except her own family, but that, Bonnie felt sure, was only because nobody realized yet what a wonderful cook Mama was or how beautifully she sewed.

Bonnie gave up her struggle with the fish flies and went back inside, where Robbie, who had not yet had his morning milk, greeted her enthusiastically. Mama was whisking a fresh panful of cookies out of the oven to add to the ones which were already laid out to cool on the kitchen table.

"One more batch and we're through." She handed a cookie to Bonnie and watched anxiously while she ate it. "I hope they're all right. If nobody wants them, there's all that flour wasted."

"When weren't your cookies all right? Wonderful, even?"

Bonnie filled a basket with crisp lettuce and red radishes from the garden, along with the first picking of green peas. Then she began laying the cookies in another basket, with brown paper between each layer to keep them from being crushed. Now that the time had actually come to ring door-bells and try to sell things to people, Bonnie felt very shaky, especially since she was going to try out a way she had thought of to show everybody how good Mama's cookies really were.

"Tommy! We're ready to go!"

"May I take my book?"

"No. You'll try to read and walk at the same time and likely fall down and spill everything."

Bonnie hurried out to the woodshed to feed Anastasia,

who was busy taking care of twelve little yellow fluffballs peeping around her feet.

"We practically have a whole flock of chickens right now," Bonnie told Tommy as they walked out the front gate with their baskets. "All we have to do is wait for them to grow up."

"I hate waiting," said Tommy. "Are we going to visit the Lewises today?"

"Maybe. I'll see how we get along."

This was what Bonnie had said every time she and Tommy had passed the Lewis house. She was nearly as curious about the Lewises as Tommy was, but somehow that word "elegant" which Cora Jane had used to describe them always frightened Bonnie away. The Lewises had arrived nearly a month before, and still Bonnie had never gone near their house.

"I've been so busy," she told herself, knowing all the time that being busy was more an excuse than it was a reason.

Just the same, she and Tommy really had been busy, earning a little here and a little there by picking strawberries and cherries, weeding an occasional garden, and even thinning peaches in the orchards which lay along the shores of the lake.

"Folks'll never hire children," Homer Hinchley had prophesied when Bonnie had set out in search of work.

"They will us," Bonnie had retorted, and a few people

had, although only after Bonnie had promised a tryout each time.

"If we don't suit you, you don't have to pay us," she always said, and so far everybody had paid.

It was not very easy to keep Tommy working as enthusiastically as Bonnie thought he should, but by arguing and persuading she had managed to keep him at it when he would much rather have been playing in the barn or the old winery.

"You're just an old Sam-in-a-Tree," Tommy grumbled.

Bonnie thought for a minute. There were times when Tommy's conversation was too much even for her.

"Simon Legree," she decided triumphantly, remembering the old copy of *Uncle Tom's Cabin* which she had been reading out loud every night after supper. "Never mind if I am a slave driver. We need every cent we can earn."

The money from their work lay hidden under Bonnie's best hat on the top shelf of her closet, ready to help pay the taxes when they came due in the winter. Not paying the taxes, Bonnie knew, was about the worst thing that could happen, because then you lost the roof over your head. Seeing how slowly the pennies came in, Bonnie had had the idea of Mama's doing sewing and baking for other people, besides the work she and Tommy could do. Bonnie sighed as she turned in at one of the summer places. She supposed the Lewis girl, whatever her first name was, never

55

had to worry about tax money or any other kind of money, either.

Nobody answered the bell at the first place where Bonnie knocked, but at the second house a cheerful woman came to the door.

"Would you like to buy some nice fresh cookies?" asked Bonnie hopefully. "Or some vegetables?"

The woman hesitated, and Bonnie whipped out a cookie from her basket.

"Have a sample," she invited. "We think Mama bakes the best cookies anywhere around."

The woman munched the cookie thoughtfully.

"It's very good," she said. "I'll take a dozen."

"Mama bakes wonderful bread, too, if you want to order any in advance. Also rolls, pies and cakes."

Before she left, Bonnie had an order for one loaf of bread for a trial and an apple pie to be delivered on Saturday in time for week-end visitors.

"You ought to try the Lewises," Bonnie's new customer advised her. "They have lots of company all summer long, and it's hard to find time for baking with a house full of people."

"I'll do that," said Bonnie politely. "And thank you for your order."

Bonnie kept on down the shore road, not having very good luck with her sales. Quite a few people were not at home or were bathing in the lake and did not want to come out even for a free sample cookie.

"Everybody that eats a cookie buys some, anyway," said Bonnie, "which proves that samples are a good idea. Let's see, we still have four dozen left and all the green peas."

"Maybe we could sell them at the store," Tommy suggested.

"We probably could, but Mr. Creedle can't pay so much because he has to make a profit when he resells them to his own customers. Oh, dear, I guess we'll have to try the Lewises, after all."

"What's the matter with the Lewises?" asked Tommy. "You aren't scared of them, are you?"

"No," said Bonnie stoutly. "I'm not scared of anybody— I guess. Maybe we ought to try the other end of the island, though."

"I'm thirsty," Tommy complained. "And I want to finish that book I found in the attic. The lady was hanging over a precipice, and I don't think she can hold on much longer."

Bonnie sighed. Tommy would never understand if she said she did not want to go to the Lewises' because they were so elegant.

"All right, then. We'll try there if we don't sell anything at this next house."

Nobody answered her knock, and Bonnie headed wearily for the Lewises'. Maybe they would not be at home, either —which was a guilty hope when Mama needed the money from Bonnie's sales so badly. Bonnie walked as fast as she could up to the front door and rang the bell. Nobody came for a few minutes, but just as she was turning away light footsteps came hurrying down the hallway.

"Oh, do come in!" A blonde girl in an embroidered white dress held the screen door open. "I've wanted to come and see you, but we've had so many visitors, and Mama always makes me help entertain them, even the old ones. Oh, and is this your brother? You come in, too. What's in the baskets?"

Bonnie felt embarrassed, because this talkative girl evidently thought they had come for a purely social visit.

"Well, we've been trying to sell some of Mama's cookies," she said hesitantly, "and green peas and—"

The girl peered into the baskets.

"Mmm! Exactly what I like. I'll ask Mama to buy some. She was just saying there wasn't anything fit to eat in the entire house. Your name's Bonnie Bishop, isn't it? Mine's Linda Lewis. Mama! Here are the new neighbors come to visit—Bonnie and Tommy Bishop."

Mrs. Lewis was a round pink-cheeked little woman with a high pompadour on which two bows of blue velvet ribbon perched precariously.

"Isn't that lovely? Why don't you girls just go right up to Linda's room? And what would you like to do, Tommy? There are some kittens out in the barn."

"Could I go in there and read?"

Tommy pointed toward the open door of the study, through which Bonnie could see tall bookcases lining the wall.

"Of course! Just help yourself to any books you want to look at. Linda, dear, what about these baskets? Are they something of ours?"

"Oh, those! Fresh cookies. Bonnie is selling them for her mother, and I thought you'd surely like some."

"Try one," Bonnie invited.

Mrs. Lewis nibbled delicately.

"Delicious! Oh, and green peas, too! Aren't we lucky you came by? We do get tired of baking in this hot weather, and Hinchley never seems to raise any decent peas."

She paid Bonnie and, still chattering, disappeared toward the kitchen. Bonnie was borne up the stairs on the flood of Linda's conversation.

"Could I go with you sometime when you sell things?" Linda ushered Bonnie into a huge bedroom with a high four-poster bed and white ruffled curtains looped back from the windows. "I think it would be loads of fun."

"Of course you can. Tommy hates to go, but I can't quite manage by myself. Are you sure you want to? It's sort of tiresome."

Bonnie was surprised to find herself telling Linda all about Pop and the tax money and the sample cookies and the sewing sign that had not brought in any customers yet.

"You ought to have samples of your mother's sewing, too," said Linda, "though I guess you couldn't carry a lot of dresses and things around with you. I do think Mama will want some sewing done, anyway. She has to get all

59

my school things made before September, and she never has any time, with all the company."

It was nearly an hour later before Bonnie came downstairs again and removed Tommy from the study.

"Let him take his book home," said Linda. "There's nothing worse than not knowing what happened in the end. Now, Bonnie, don't forget to stop by for me the very next time you go out selling things." She gave Bonnie's arm a little squeeze. "Oh, I'm so glad there's a girl practically next door! I'm almost not going to miss my friends in Chicago at all!"

Homer Hinchley stepped out to the road just as Bonnie and Tommy passed his house.

"Thought I told you to stay away from the Lewises," he growled.

"Tell away!" Bonnie tossed her head. "Linda asked us to come back any time we want to, so there!"

Hinchley looked crestfallen, but only for a minute.

"You got a license to peddle all that stuff?" he demanded.

"Have you got one yourself?" asked Bonnie. "I saw you peddling strawberries just the other day. Besides, I don't think I need a license."

"You don't." Mr. Pippett's horses, Albert and Almira, had halted beside her in the road, and for a minute Bonnie imagined it was Albert who had spoken. Mr. Pippett leaned from the wagon seat. "Don't have to have a license to peddle home-grown stuff." He looked coldly at Hinchley. "Have to think up some other way to devil 'em, won't you?"

Hinchley glared and stomped back into his house.

"Thank you," said Bonnie to Mr. Pippett. "I wish I knew why he hates us so much."

Mr. Pippett shrugged.

"Hard telling. Natural cussedness, most likely, the same thing that made him take that desk of yours."

"Then he did take it!" cried Bonnie.

"I couldn't prove it," said Mr. Pippett, "but I've been asking around some. Some years back, Hinchley told Mr. Creedle down at the store to order him a desk from over on the mainland, and then right after your Great-Uncle Eben died Hinchley came into the store and said never mind, he'd been able to pick up a desk secondhand. When I saw that desk gone, I put two and two together and got anyway four—and maybe five. Hinchley's like that; he'd lift something out of an empty house if he was sure he could get away with it. Probably thought nobody'd be coming back that'd know the difference. People hardly ever go to his house for anything, and if they do he doesn't let 'em in, so nobody'd be seeing the desk there."

"Then why did he bring it back?" Bonnie wondered.

"Afraid I'd start the constable hunting for it, I expect," said Mr. Pippett. "Whatever it was, my advice to you folks is to stay as far away from Hinchley as possible."

"Don't worry," said Bonnie. "We don't like him a bit better than he does us."

61

"He doesn't like anybody. He had a real good job with a printer in Canada a few years ago, but he couldn't get along with the folks over there any better than he can here. Well, no use wasting pity on him. He owns some property around and has money in the bank—more than you'd think."

"Where did he get it," asked Bonnie, always interested in ways to get money, "aside from stealing people's furniture?"

"Couldn't say for sure. Fur business must be better than any of us suspected." He clucked to Albert and Almira. "Well, see you later."

Not until she was back home with the empty baskets sitting triumphantly on the kitchen table did Bonnie realize that Linda's elegance had not been the least bit frightening and that even Mr. Lewis, glimpsed through the parlor door, had not been as terrifying as "a big man from Chicago" might be expected to be.

"What did Linda wear?" asked Cora Jane. "What did their parlor look like? Was it very grand? Were you scared?"

"Well, she had on embroidered linen." Bonnie looked down ruefully at her own plain gingham. "And the parlor had a lot of gilt-edged mirrors and a satin sofa and brocade curtains. But I wasn't scared at all, and Linda's going with me the next time I sell cookies." She paused for breath. "Where's Mama?"

"She's in the parlor. She's been there a couple of hours, just sitting. I don't think she feels very well."

Bonnie rushed into the parlor. Mama was sitting wanly on the sofa with her hands clenched in her lap.

"Mama! What's the matter?"

Mama silently held out a long white envelope.

"Who's it from? What does it say?" Bonnie looked at the return address in the corner—World-Wide Steamship Lines. "Oh!"

"I—I didn't open it," Mama quavered. "I thought I'd wait for you."

Bonnie patted her mother's shoulder. World-Wide Steamship Lines was the company that owned the *Nancy Belle,* Pop's old ship.

"Well, somebody has to open it!" Bonnie ripped open the envelope and spread out the letter inside. "Oh, dear, nothing's changed. They just wrote to say there isn't anything new to tell and to ask if we're getting along all right."

She handed the letter to Mama to read and thought for the hundredth time of all the things which might have happened to keep Pop from coming home. Most likely he had been sick somewhere—very sick—and then of course the boat had gone and when he got well there would be no quick way to get home, because he would not have much money and maybe for a while he could not get a job to pay his way. Bonnie looked at Mama, who was staring tearfully off into space again.

"Just don't you fret, Mama," she said. "Pop'll be back all right. Why, he's probably on his way right now."

As she sliced cold boiled potatoes into the pan to fry for supper, she tried to keep from turning all these things over and over in her mind and racking her brain for an answer that would not come. The only thing she could do anything about, actually, was helping to keep the family clothed and fed. Bonnie brightened. It all looked just a little easier, now that Linda was going to help her, even though it was only by going around with her to sell Mama's pastries.

The very next day, Linda appeared at the front door, asked for Mama, and said her mother would like a few loaves of bread and a chocolate cake if it was convenient.

"She wants to talk about some sewing, too," said Linda, "only not until this batch of company leaves. I do declare, before one set of people goes home another set is coming in the door. Bonnie, can we sell cookies tomorrow?"

She left in a great rush with some cinnamon rolls, fresh out of the oven, and a handful of rosy radishes. Bonnie smiled after her.

"Isn't she darling? So—so sunshiny!"

Linda continued to be sunshiny during the days which followed. Chattering every minute, she trotted beside Bonnie on their selling expeditions. She badgered all kinds of people into buying Mama's baking and took repeat orders from the customers two and sometimes three days a week. She made little speeches about Mama's sewing, urging everybody she saw to have a few dresses made. Still, nobody seemed really interested in that branch of the business.

"It's too silly," Linda complained almost daily. "If they saw your mother's work in some store window in Chicago they'd rush right in and buy it." She fingered an embroidered petticoat which Mama had just finished. "Look at that! You can't get anything that pretty anywhere else!"

"I wonder," said Mama after Linda had left one day, "whether we could do your hair in curls like hers."

"My hair's straight as a stick," Bonnie protested.

"We could put it up on rags. And I know I could copy that dress she had on today. There isn't anything to it, really, except those pleats at the shoulders."

Bonnie shook her head sadly.

"No use trying to make me like Linda," she said. "I don't have the looks or the disposition, either."

For instance, she could not imagine Linda's ever speaking to Hinchley the way Bonnie had the day she had found him leaning against the barn and talking to a wide-eyed Tommy and Cora Jane.

"Yes, sir, that winery's haunted, especially them two cellars. Wailing and crying fit to stand your hair on end. Ghost of a drowneded girl carrying a bloody dagger and walking through the walls like they wasn't even there!"

"Ghost of a muskrat, most likely!" Bonnie had cried indignantly. "And don't you ever let me catch you scaring Tommy and Cora Jane again with all that trash!" She had turned to the children. "Don't you believe a word he says—not a single word."

Linda, she supposed, would have managed to speak nicely to Hinchley even then. Bonnie had been taught to speak nicely, too, but she could not help wondering whether Linda's manners would have held up if Hinchley had been as horrid to her as he had to Bonnie. She wanted very much to tell Linda all about her troubles with Hinchley, but she hated to be a tale-teller and anyway Pop had always told her, "Fight your own battles. It's no fun having somebody else win for you."

Bonnie went to her room early that night, turning out the lamp and curling up in the old rocking chair by the window, with Robbie purring on her lap. She could see all the way down to the lake, where the winery was a gray mass in the moonlight. The beam from the lighthouse on Steppingstone Island swept slowly across the sky, back and forth, back and forth.

It was easier to think at night this way, with nobody saying anything, and Bonnie needed to think a lot if she was going to figure out a way to get some sewing for Mama—right now, too, while the summer people were still here. Asking wouldn't do it, because she and Linda had asked practically everybody on the island. It all came back to the same thing: people liked to see what they were getting. It had been easy enough with the cookies, but, as Linda said, Bonnie could hardly run up and down the

66

island with a stack of dresses over her arm—so floppy and uninteresting.

Bonnie sighed and idly noted the lighthouse beam sweeping across the winery. Part of the beam seemed to be staying behind—a tiny splinter of light that did not leave the winery when the rest of the beam did. Bonnie squinted her eyes and looked more intently. The light flickered and moved and then went out entirely, to Bonnie's relief.

"Either ghosts or people," Pop would have said, "and no help for it either way."

Bonnie naturally preferred people; they filled out their clothes so much better. Suddenly Bonnie sat up straight in her chair, spilling Robbie onto the floor.

"I do believe I've got it!" she told her indignant pet. "Just wait until tomorrow! I'll have enough sewing orders to keep Mama busy all summer!"

More Flies

CHAPTER FIVE

I T'S SISSY STUFF, and I'm not going to do it!" Tommy glared at Bonnie and Linda and at the fancy new shirt which was lying on the bed on top of his Sunday suit. "Who wants to look like Little Lord Saunterboy?"

"Little Lord Fauntleroy. And you are, too, going to do it." Bonnie fixed him with a stern eye. "You get right into those clothes, and no back talk! You know we have to earn money if we're going to eat next winter."

Linda gave Tommy a sympathetic smile.

"I don't blame you a bit for not wanting to do it, being a boy and all, but I don't know how in the world we'll manage without you," she said. "If all the ladies could see what lovely boys' shirts and suits your mother can make, I just know we could get her lots of sewing to do. And with real live models—" Her voice trailed sadly off. "Oh, well, we'll have Cora Jane, anyway."

Cora Jane slid into the room, resplendent in pink embroidered linen with a huge matching bow in her hair. Bonnie was wearing smocked plaid gingham and Linda had on the ruffled blue organdy that Mama had just finished for her. Tommy looked from one to the other.

"I can't get ready if you're all going to stand right here in my room," he said finally. "Just remember, though, I'm only doing it for Mama—and because Linda wants me to."

Linda smiled at him.

"I think it's awfully sweet of you," she said, "and I do wish I had a brother exactly like you."

"Whew!" said Bonnie as they waited in the dining room. "It's a lucky thing you were here. He'd never in the world have done it for me."

"Mama says you catch more flies with honey than you do with vinegar," said Linda lightly.

Bonnie stole a guilty look at her friend. Unhappily she remembered how sharply she had been speaking to Tommy before Linda had smoothed everything over with her gentle talk. No matter how hard she tried to act like Linda, it seemed that sharp words came naturally out of Bonnie's mouth when things did not go to suit her, even though she knew perfectly well that honey did catch more flies than vinegar. The trouble was that she never seemed to remember it when the time came.

"There! We're all ready." Bonnie took special pains to smile at Tommy as he came out of his room with his hair slicked down and his buttoned shoes blacked just as carefully as they were for Sunday. "Oh, I do hope it works!"

Bonnie had a sinking sensation as she rang the doorbell at the first house past the Lewises', where she had heard that some new people had arrived for the rest of the summer.

"I should have brought some cookies or a cake," she whispered faintly to Linda. "Maybe they'd want to buy that, even if they don't want any sewing done."

"One thing at a time," Linda advised. "We can try them on baked goods later."

The door opened, and Bonnie went nervously into her speech without even looking to see who was standing in the dim hall inside.

"Good morning, ma'am," she began. "I'm Bonnie Bishop from just down the road, and I wonder if you want any fine sewing done. My mother can make boys' shirts and suits—step up, Tommy, and show the lady— also girls' and ladies' dresses, embroidered or plain. This ruffled organdy is nice or the embroidered linen or my own gingham, which would be wonderful for school in the fall."

"Ruffled organdy." A deep bass voice answered her. "I want ruffled organdy to go with my beard."

Stricken, Bonnie stared up into the face of a huge man, who did indeed have a beard, a big red bushy one that hid most of his face.

"I—I—" she began feebly, but no more words came.

The big man burst into a roar of laughter.

"Don't look so scared! I'm not going to eat you, seeing I had my breakfast already. Hilda! Come quick now! We have a fashion show right on our own doorstep!"

A blonde woman almost as big as her husband joined him on the porch.

"Do you think your mother can make shirts big enough for me—like a tent, almost?" Mr. Redbeard asked.

"Yes, sir," said Bonnie. "She can make anything. And you can buy good madras at the general store. Some real pretty patterns."

"Colors to go with my beard, maybe?" The big man grinned at the children. "This afternoon Hilda and I go and buy the material, then we bring it to your mother, along with an old shirt to use for a pattern. She won't believe, maybe, how much material it takes."

Bonnie stared, enchanted, at her first customer.

"I certainly thank you," she said fervently, herding Tommy and Cora Jane ahead of her down the steps. "I know you'll be pleased."

"When they come, your mother can give them some tea and cookies," Linda suggested. "That way they'll get a chance to sample her baked goods, and most likely they'll order some. Just be sure the sign is right by the front gate so they can't miss seeing it."

For the rest of the morning, Bonnie was careful to take a good look at each prospective customer before she began to talk. Some people acted as though the whole project were just a free entertainment, but others seemed really interested in seeing Mama's beautiful handwork.

At noon, when the four young models staggered wearily back home, three more people had promised to stop by and have Mama sew something for them. Bonnie began counting the orders on her fingers.

"Three little girls' dresses from that house on the corner, one shirtwaist for the lady in the green house, and a summer suit for Mrs. Cameron's little boy, not counting Mr. Redbeard's shirts."

It was not as much as she had expected, but at least it proved that the idea of having models was a good one.

"People like to think things over," Linda assured her. "You'll see, lots more folks will be dropping around to talk to your mother about patterns and dress goods all summer long. And we haven't been to half the places yet, either."

Tommy groaned faintly but brightened when the girls told him his modeling was over for that day.

"I hope you won't mind going again tomorrow," said Linda, smiling as Tommy took off his shoes and stockings and wiggled his toes luxuriously. "Morning's much the best time, and of course we want to get the summer people into the notion as soon as possible. We can save the island folks for later, seeing they're here all year anyway."

Tommy nodded agreeably and went to his room to finish a book which he had been reading.

"Let's go down to the winery," Bonnie suggested to Linda. "You can wear one of my old dresses so you won't spoil your organdy."

"Bring a candle," said Linda, "so we can see in the cellars."

Linda was almost as fond of the winery as Bonnie was. The girls spent many afternoons there, sitting and talking either on the sunny doorstep or on one of the wide window sills which overlooked the lake. They could see the islands clearly today—all the American ones and even a few of the Canadian ones. Bonnie leaned out to watch a sailboat which was going briskly by with its sails frosting-white in the sunshine.

"Maybe it's going to Canada," she sighed. "Imagine—a whole different country, right over there."

"It's not much different from here. At least Rock Island isn't. We went on the excursion boat once, and people say Mr. Hinchley walks over sometimes in the winter when the lake is frozen good and solid." Linda stood up suddenly. "Let's go down in the cellars. Somebody might have come and buried some treasure since last week."

Bonnie tried obediently to think of glittering heaps of gold doubloons and pieces of eight, but instead she pictured weary pirates holding their aching backs as they pried up the heavy stone slabs of the floor to scoop out a hiding place for their treasure.

The girls gave the first cellar only a passing glance. The second one was always much more interesting because it was so dark. It looked very strange and mysterious, even though so far the girls had found nothing but emptiness.

"Light the candle," said Linda. "We don't want to miss anything."

"The day we find anything exciting down here will be the same day I find the secret drawer in Pop's desk," Bonnie declared disgustedly, following Linda in her circuit of the cavernous cellar.

75

"There!" Linda suddenly pounced. "I told you there was treasure!"

She pressed something small and furry into Bonnie's hand. Bonnie screamed and dropped whatever it was, and Linda laughed.

"Nothing but a little piece of muskrat fur. What's so scary about that?"

"I was just surprised."

Bonnie looked down at the scrap of silvery-brown fur at her feet. She could not help thinking of the ghost of a muskrat which she had mentioned so jeeringly to Hinchley. It was all nonsense, of course, but still Bonnie shivered a little and did not pick up the bit of fur from the dusty stone floor. She wondered how the muskrat got down here. Any sensible muskrat would stay in his cool mound of roots and rushes out in the marsh and not go prowling around wine cellars.

"We might try getting this open again," said Linda.

She held the candle high and looked carefully at the old door on the lake side. Bonnie tugged at the hasp.

"Tommy tries every time we're down here, but it just won't. It's swelled up tight on account of the dampness."

"It ought to be all rotted away," said Linda. "Everything else is—front doors and window frames and everything."

Bonnie had never wondered about the door in that way, although she had once waded out a little way in the lake to see whether she could find any trace of the unloading dock which must once have been just outside that door.

Some little stubs of piling had been all she could find to mark the spot.

"Let's go back upstairs," said Bonnie, who never liked to stay down in the cellars very long and especially not now, since Linda had stirred up the ghost of the muskrat.

"You know what?" Linda darted off in still another direction in her conversation. "I'm going to have a birthday party in August just before we go home, and I hope you'll come. Mama wants your mother to make me a new dress for it. Pale-blue taffeta with a lace collar. She's going to order the material from Chicago."

"I'd love to come. I haven't been to a party since we moved here."

Bonnie tried to make her voice sound enthusiastic, although she was already wondering what she could wear to such an elegant affair. Silk would be perfect, but where could she possibly get a silk dress? Mama had one—the pale-green satin which she had been married in—but Bonnie never expected to have one of her own until she grew up. She would have to think of something for a present besides—something that didn't cost much, if anything. She did get tired of counting every penny and then wondering where the next one was coming from. How wonderful it would be to walk into a store and, just once, buy something without even asking the price!

Bonnie was so silent at supper that Mama asked her if she had a fever. Bonnie shook her head. It would only make Mama feel sad if Bonnie said she was worrying be-

77

37717

cause she did not have a silk dress to wear to Linda's party. After all, Linda knew every dress in Bonnie's wardrobe and she would never expect Bonnie to appear in any such sudden splendor as a silk dress. Still, it would be lovely to be a credit to Linda, so that her other guests would say, "Isn't that Bishop girl nicely dressed? An aristocratic old island family, they tell me."

At this high-flown thought, Bonnie could hardly keep from snickering. No matter how she dressed, she was not going to be anybody but plain Bonnie Bishop, who peddled baked goods and weeded carrots and argued with Homer Hinchley—none of which could possibly be considered aristocratic activities. It would be better to concentrate on Linda's present, which was probably going to be even more of a problem than the dress.

Bonnie finished the dishes, wiped her hands absentmindedly on the kitchen curtains instead of the hand towel, and went into her room to escape from Tommy, who was bent on telling her the complete plot of the book he had just finished. In a few minutes, she heard the front door open and then Mama's voice, breathless with surprise. Cora Jane came scampering into Bonnie's room.

"Mama wants you to come into the parlor. Mr. Hinchley's here. Just wait until you see him!"

Hinchley was perched uneasily on the very edge of the slippery horsehair sofa. He was shaved, his hair was combed except for a cowlick which stuck straight up from the back of his head, and he was wearing a rusty black suit, a pair of snub-nosed tan shoes, and a pink shirt topped by a celluloid collar and a drooping black tie.

"No need to call your daughter," he was remarking as Bonnie slid into the room. "Just a little business matter we can settle between ourselves as easy as not."

Mama gestured nervously for Bonnie to sit down.

"I wouldn't want to decide anything without Bonnie," she said, "so if you'll—

"Well, I—uh—" Hinchley tugged at his collar. "I—uh— thought I might be able to find some work for your three if you could—uh—spare 'em. Gardening and such." He added what was obviously a painful touch. "I'd—uh—pay the going rate, even if they aren't but just children. Neighbors and—uh—neighbors."

Bonnie stared at Hinchley with her mouth slightly ajar. Seeing him dressed up and also polite was almost too much of a shock for one day. What in the world did he really want, behind all this mush-mouthed talk of work and neighbors? Bonnie was on the point of asking straight out, but then she remembered about catching more flies with honey than with vinegar.

"I think that's lovely of you," she said in a voice which she tried to make as much like Linda's as possible. "We'll do our very best to please."

Hinchley eased himself gingerly back on the horsehair sofa and gave his dingy fingernails a minute inspection.

"I was wondering," he said in an offhand manner, "if

79

you might not want to sell that land where the old wine cellar is. No use to you that I can see."

"Well—" Mama began.

"No use to you, either," Bonnie broke in. "What do you want it for?"

"Storage," said Hinchley vaguely. "I've got a raft of odds and ends lying around. My barn's full and all the sheds. I need to clear out a place for my furs so's I'll be ready when the trapping season starts. Have to stretch the pelts and this and that. Takes space."

"How did you manage before now?" asked Bonnie.

Hinchley seemed not to hear her.

"All I'd need would be a door so's I could lock the place up, and some windows to keep the weather out." He turned to Mama. "What do you say?"

"We couldn't sell it," said Bonnie. "Pop owns this place, and we—we can't reach him just now."

"Never will reach him, either." Hinchley turned again to Mama. "He won't be back, and you know it well's I do. Them foreign places—he'd be back before now if he was coming."

"He'll be here." Bonnie bit back the angry words which she felt coming to her lips. "And he wouldn't want us to sell the winery."

"Nobody asked you," said Hinchley. "I'm talking to your ma. Will you sell it, ma'am, or won't you?"

Mama shook her head.

"I'm sorry, but I don't see how we could, not legally.

80

No, we wouldn't rent it, either, not until we—we know for sure about my husband."

Bonnie went over to stand beside Mama, who looked as though she were about to cry. Hinchley, red of face, tried to get up from the sofa, but the rug skidded under his feet and landed him with a thud on the floor. Bonnie swallowed a giggle as he rolled over on all fours before finally struggling to his feet.

"Nothing to laugh at, that I can see," he mumbled. "Should have known better than try to help you out, anyway. Bishops always were too big for their boots!"

"More flies with honey than with vinegar," Bonnie chanted grimly over and over in her mind. "More flies—"

Hinchley's face seemed red enough to set his celluloid collar afire as he yanked open the front door, which always stuck at the sill.

"Changed my mind about them jobs," he rumbled. "No use doing favors for folks that won't do one back."

The door shuddered as he closed it behind him, and Bonnie could hear his heels pounding angrily along the brick walk.

"That man!" Bonnie exploded. "Going to do us a favor! I can just imagine!" She patted Mama's shoulder comfortingly. "My, I do wish Linda could have heard me this time! All honey and never a drop of vinegar. Not that it got us any flies." She sighed ruefully. "Oh, well, who wants flies?"

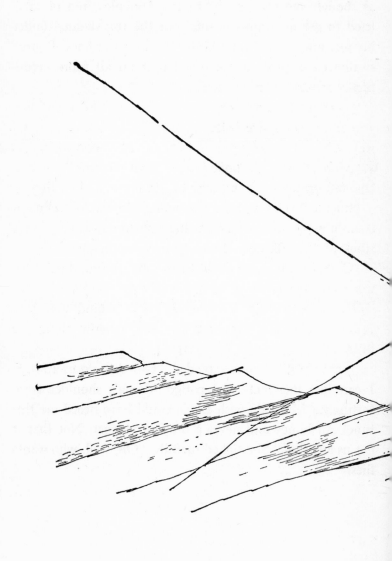

Found: One Flashlight

CHAPTER SIX

Bonnie stood in front of the dim old mirror of her dresser and admired the new and different Bonnie who smiled back at her. This Bonnie, ready to go to Linda's party, wore long curls, products of a night spent tossing on the knobs made by rag curlers. She nervously patted her hair and wished she could be sure it did not intend to collapse into its natural straight condition right in the middle of the party.

"You look beautiful!" Cora Jane stared admiringly at her sister. "When I get asked to a party, do you think Mama will make me a silk dress, too?"

"I wouldn't be surprised. There's a whole other pair of those curtains left."

Bonnie frowned a little, thinking of her dress, made from an old pair of taffeta curtains which she had found tucked into the bottom of a trunk in the attic. The dress was beautiful—a soft rose which set off Bonnie's black hair—but Mama had not wanted to make it.

"That material might be thirty years old," she had protested. "It'll probably split the first move you make. And anyway, you've drummed up so much sewing and baking business for me I hardly know whether I'm going or coming."

"Mama," Bonnie had begged, "please, please try. I just know it will hold together. It has to; it's so pretty."

Mama had thrown up her hands.

"All right. Figure out how you want it made, and I'll do my best, though I don't fancy all that work for something that won't last any time at all."

Seeing herself in the mirror, Bonnie was glad that she had been able to convince Mama. The skirt of her dress fell in soft folds, and above the round neckline the string of crystal beads which Pop had given Mama long years ago shone like diamonds.

"I'll just remember not to make any sudden moves." Bonnie bent carefully over the bottom dresser drawer, where Linda's present lay. "Cora Jane, you do think Linda will like it, don't you?"

She lifted out the embroidered linen collar over which she had toiled every day for weeks. She looked proudly at the scalloped edges, the French knots arranged like little clusters of flowers, and the tiny sprays of green leaves. Cora Jane helped tie the collar up in a handkerchief box with a pink bow on top.

"It's a beautiful present," said Cora Jane. "She can wear it all winter with her wool dresses."

Thinking of winter reminded Bonnie that in just a week the Lewises would be closing their house and going back to Chicago.

"I'll write every single week," Linda had promised, "and anyway it won't be so terribly long until next summer."

No matter what Linda said, Bonnie knew that it was going to be a long, long wait until next summer, even with

school beginning in a couple of weeks to keep Bonnie twice
as busy as she already was.

"It's time to start to the party." Mama stuck her head
in the doorway. "Seeing it's still light, you may go by yourself, but I'll send Tommy to bring you home. And you
better hurry now; it looks like rain." She twisted her hands
nervously. "Oh, Bonnie, I do hope that dress holds together."

"Of course it will hold together."

Bonnie kissed Mama with a feeling of impatience. Mama
did worry so about things that hardly ever happened. Bonnie felt very elegant as she walked sedately down the road,
looking sideways at Homer Hinchley's place as she passed.
It would be nice to know what he really had wanted of
their winery. All that talk about storage space was perfectly
silly, because even now, with fifty baskets of peaches standing on the barn floor ready to cross to the mainland on
the noon boat tomorrow, his barn looked almost empty—
full of fresh air and not much else. Hinchley had not been
very bothersome lately, maybe because he knew that Bonnie and Linda were such good friends, but Bonnie was not
sure what was going to happen during the winter when
Linda was gone.

Feeling suddenly very unsure of herself, Bonnie turned
in at Linda's gate. A little knot of girls on the porch looked
at her silently, but Linda rushed forward, cried, "Oh, here's
Bonnie. Now we can begin!" and swept her around the
circle to make the introductions. All the girls were from

the summer families, and one of them was wearing a dress which Mama had made for her. Bonnie was happy to see that her own dress was as pretty as anybody's there, and again she was glad that she had out-argued Mama about making it in the first place.

Out of respect for the possible frailty of her dress, Bonnie sat cautiously on the sofa while Linda, surrounded by billowing tissue paper, opened her pile of presents.

"Oh, Bonnie, it's lovely!" cried Linda when she came to Bonnie's embroidered collar. "I'll think of you every time I wear it."

Bonnie blushed and wished she could think of something more graceful to say in return than an abrupt "Glad you like it." She was relieved when the games started and everybody concentrated on them instead of on each other. Bonnie gingerly took her turn at tossing beans into the bottle and spinning the plate, being careful not to move too hastily. She would much rather have romped as carelessly as the others, but at least she had the consolation of knowing that her precious dress looked very handsome against the blue satin of the sofa.

Mrs. Lewis threw open the folding doors to the dining room, and the girls flocked in to admire a table festooned with crepe paper and centered with a huge pink-and-white birthday cake.

"Linda may blow out her candles, and then we'll cut the cake," said Mrs. Lewis. "Just all step up and find your places."

Bonnie gave a sigh of relief. The games were over, and nothing could possibly happen to her dress while she was sitting quietly at the table with a dish of strawberry ice cream, a slice of birthday cake, and a tall glass of lemonade in front of her. She could probably wear the dress to a dozen more parties and then hand it down to be made over for Cora Jane.

A plump girl—Bonnie would have said just plain "fat" but she remembered that Linda always said "plump" instead—reached for a dish of mints and joggled Bonnie's glass of lemonade with her elbow. Bonnie made a desperate grab to keep the glass from overturning. She heard an ominous ripping sound across the middle of her back.

"What was that?" asked the plump girl.

"What was what?" Bonnie felt a sudden draft across her shoulders and leaned firmly against the back of the chair. "Such lovely cake, isn't it?"

With every breath, Bonnie could feel the ripped material giving way a little more. She looked desperately at the circle of faces. The door to the kitchen was directly behind her if she could only get through it without anybody's seeing her dress. There was a little stir as everybody started to get up and go back into the parlor.

"My goodness gracious, look over there!"

Bonnie pointed excitedly toward the hall doorway. While everybody turned to look, she leaped to her feet and backed rapidly into the kitchen. She scurried past the Lewises' surprised hired girl and on out the back door.

"It's rainin', Miss Bonnie," the hired girl called after her, "and it looks to me like you've split your dress straight down the back."

Bonnie ran even faster. Rain poured down on her head, and she could feel her wonderful curls turning into lank straight strands. She tore past Homer Hinchley's place and tiptoed at last around to her own back door and into the safety of her room.

She threw herself on the bed and began to cry. Her beautiful dress was ruined, her curls were gone, and she had made a spectacle of herself at Linda's party. She could imagine what Mama would say if she ever heard that Bonnie had left without saying "Thank you for the lovely time." Even with a split dress, a person was supposed to have some manners. Linda would just have laughed and said, "Well, I do declare," if it had been her dress, but of course if Linda's dress had split it would not have been because it was made out of an old pair of curtains—which was what really made all the difference. That and the fact that Mama had told Bonnie from the first what would happen and Bonnie had been too stubborn to listen.

"Nothing stubborner than a mule—except a woman," Pop would have said, grinning at Mama while he said it. Bonnie began to cry harder. Pop was so far away and getting farther all the time. Cora Jane and Tommy and Mama spoke of him less and less, and even to Bonnie he sometimes seemed like a long-ago dream that was beginning to fade. She shut her eyes and made his face come back, clear and sharp, for just a minute.

"Bonnie!" Tommy came puffing into her room. "My, I'm glad you got home! There's somebody in the winery. I can see the light moving around. Hurry up, and maybe we can catch them."

"You start on," said Bonnie, "but don't go too close without me. I'll be there as soon as I get this dress off."

She hung her wet, torn dress far back on a hanger in her closet. There was just a chance that Mama might not have to find out right away what had happened—maybe not until the next time there was a party. Bonnie could hear Mama in the parlor now, playing songs on the wheezy old organ and singing to herself, so softly that Bonnie could barely hear her. The only times that Mama had ever sung out good and loud were when Pop used to sing, too, bending over the cottage organ they had had in Boston and laughing as Mama's fingers flew to keep up.

Bonnie let herself quietly out of the house and started toward the winery. The rain had nearly stopped, and the moon was trying to come out through a hole in the clouds.

"Psst!" Tommy's head popped up from behind a bush just a little way from the winery. "See that?"

Bonnie peered through the gloom. There was certainly a dim light moving in the winery—so dim that Bonnie thought it must be casting its faint glow up the stairs from down in one of the cellars.

"Let's move up by the window," Bonnie whispered.

"When they come out, it'll be through the door, and nobody'll even know we're here."

The children huddled close to the window, peering into the inner darkness. Once Bonnie thought she could hear the faint murmur of voices, but then she decided it might be the lake waves lapping on the shore.

"We can't see anything from out here," Tommy complained. "How about my going inside for a minute? I can stand on the stairs and run away whenever I see the light coming."

"If you're going, I'm going too. And don't make a sound, no matter what happens."

Bonnie shivered a little as they tiptoed across the big room and flattened themselves against the wall part way down the stairs. The light was a little brighter now, and Bonnie was sure this time of the murmur of voices—maybe three people talking—and of the sound of footsteps. Suddenly Tommy clutched Bonnie's arm.

"I—I think I'm going to—" He gave a convulsive gasp. "KA-CHOO!"

A muffled exclamation came from the cellar. The light disappeared, there was the sound of hurrying feet, and Bonnie heard a thud and a splashing sound. After a paralyzed moment, she pulled Tommy away from the stairway.

"Run!" she hissed. "They'll be coming up right this way!"

The children retreated to their old place outside the window, where there was a sheltering bush under which they could duck if need be. Bonnie held her breath so she could listen better, but there was only silence in the winery. The light did not go back on, and Bonnie was sure that nobody had come through the doorway, which was now bathed in moonlight. Suddenly Bonnie remembered the splashing sound.

She guided Tommy silently around the winery to the shore. Just a little way out, barely visible even in the moonlight, a boat was being rowed cautiously away from land. In a moment the motor sputtered and caught, and the boat chugged out into the lake.

"Now how did they manage that?" Bonnie wondered. "I don't think anybody could get out that little window in the second cellar and then drop down to the shore. Of course there's the old door, but it'd take a charge of dynamite to get that open."

"I'm going right down and see," said Tommy.

"You are not! It's dark as pitch down there. They're gone now, anyway. We'll come and look first thing in the morning."

The children managed to get home a few minutes before Mama came into the kitchen to remind Tommy to go to Linda's for his sister. Bonnie was already in her bathrobe placidly brushing her hair.

"You're back already!" Mama exclaimed.

"It was a perfectly lovely party," said Bonnie, trying to look both gay and innocent. "My dress was the prettiest one there and the games were fun and Linda just loved her collar."

Mama bent to kiss Bonnie good night.

"I'm so glad," she said. "You have to have a little fun once in a while."

"I do have fun." Bonnie patted Mama's hand. "I have fun all the time."

In the morning Bonnie and Tommy hurried down to the winery, which lay calm and silent in the summer sunshine. The ivy swayed gently in the breeze, which brought the half-fish, half-water smell of the lake to Bonnie's nostrils.

Tommy lit the lantern which he had brought from the house and the children hurried down into the cellar, flashing the lantern rays against the walls and into all the corners. In the second cellar, they took an especially careful look at the window, which turned out to be so small that nobody but a baby could crawl through it, and at the door, which remained hopelessly stuck.

"Magic," said Bonnie. "They must have flown through the keyhole—only there isn't any keyhole. Tommy, flash the lantern over this way a minute." She bent and picked up something. "A flashlight. So somebody really was here!"

"Let's hold it for ransom," said Tommy.

"It'll be better to pretend we never saw it," Bonnie decided. "Nobody'd be foolish enough to ask us for it and let us know they were snooping around down here. Let's put a mark on it so we'll know it again and just leave it

right where we found it. Then if whoever it was comes and
gets it we might be able to trace it."

"How?" asked Tommy.

"Well, we could go around and borrow everybody's
flashlight and hunt for the mark."

Tommy looked disgusted.

"That isn't very exciting. I read in a book once how you
can get fingerprints off things and catch criminals."

"How could we get any fingerprints off the people to
match up with the fingerprints on the flashlight?" asked
Bonnie impatiently.

"It wouldn't be any harder than thinking up reasons to
borrow people's flashlights," Tommy complained, but he
obediently unscrewed the end of the flashlight and
scratched a tiny "B" just under the edge. Then he screwed
the end back on and laid the flashlight back in the dark
corner where Bonnie had found it.

"I have to go over to Linda's," said Bonnie. "I'll be right
back."

It was going to be hard to walk into Linda's and explain
why she had run away from the party, but Bonnie knew
she had to do it. As it turned out, it was not as bad as
she had feared.

She explained carefully to Mrs. Lewis, who patted Bonnie's shoulder and told her to forget the whole thing. Linda
giggled and said, "That pointing out toward the hall was
just wonderful. Everybody was so busy looking that they
never even saw you go. I just hope I remember that trick

94

sometime when I need it. Oh, Bonnie, I'm going to miss you so!"

With her apologies made, Bonnie was able to start school the next week with an easy mind except for her usual wondering about the unknown owner of the flashlight.

"Bonnie Bishop," the teacher said one day, "what are you thinking about? I asked you twice what the capital of Turkey is."

Bonnie hastily returned to the present.

"I'm sorry, ma'am. I—I guess I don't know."

Miss Burton frowned at her and made her stay after school to write "I will pay attention" one hundred times on the blackboard. Bonnie never told Miss Burton what she had been thinking about—not only the mysterious visitors to the winery but also Linda's being gone and the amount of money the Bishops still had to save up to pay their taxes. They had almost enough, if nobody had to spend any money for anything unexpected.

The trouble was that it was hard to earn money on the island now that all the summer people were gone. Mama's baking business was practically at an end, because the islanders baked their own pies and cakes except for special occasions. Mama was doing only a little sewing—a wool serge suit for Mr. Creedle, the storekeeper, who was so large that it was hard for him to buy anything ready-made, and a red velvet dress for little Veronica Smith, who was going to be flower girl at her cousin's wedding on the mainland. Bonnie was grateful when Mr. Pippett stopped his wagon on the road one day in November and asked Bonnie whether the children could come and pick the last of the grapes for him.

"Looks like a good hard freeze is due almost any day now," he said, "and those grapes did get ahead of me, so I'd take it as a favor if you'd come when you can—after school or any time you can spare."

"We'll be there tomorrow."

Bonnie had long ago stopped trying to thank Mr. Pippett for the favors which he said they were doing for him when really it was the other way around. This favor turned out to be an especially important one because the money from picking the grapes made up almost the amount lacking for the taxes—for the December taxes, that is. That meant that in June—or July, at the latest—the Bishops would have to rake up more money for the taxes for the other half of the year. Sewing, baking, vegetables, odd jobs—Bonnie counted them over in her mind and hoped that she and Mama would be able to manage.

It would have been so much less worrisome to pay for the whole year at one time, the way Pop had done, and be able to relax for a little while. Bonnie sighed and tucked the money away in her favorite hiding place under her best hat, ready to be sent to the tax collector as soon as the first bill came.

Walking to school as the days grew shorter and chillier, Bonnie could not help feeling sad to see Linda's house shuttered and empty. Even the constable did not come around to keep an eye on the Lewis place as he did on the other summer houses, because that was supposed to be Hinchley's job.

The truth was that Bonnie missed Linda even more than she had expected to. The children at school were friendly enough, but none of them were as much fun as Linda, and all of them had their own friends whom they had known time out of mind. Bonnie had never thought of herself as being especially timid but still she hesitated to push in where she was not sure she was wanted.

"Bishops always were too proud to ask favors," Pop used to say sometimes. "A pity, too, when there are so many people who like to help other folks out."

Bonnie thought it was pleasure in doing a favor which had brought Mama out of the house so often during the fall to help sew for the heathen. The minister's wife had started it by knocking on the door one day and saying, "I want to ask your help, Mrs. Bishop. Would you come to the church and give us some advice about our sewing tomorrow afternoon? The ladies are having trouble getting some shirt collars to lie right, and they tell me you're a real expert."

Mama looked flustered, but she smiled and promised to come. After that, she went one afternoon every week to help remodel old clothes or to sew new ones for the missionary barrels which the island ladies sent to distant parts of the world. Bonnie thought that the heathen must have been surprised at some of the items which came out of those wooden barrels—a suit of long red underwear, a skirt made of some striped red-and-green portieres, a wide-brimmed beaver hat with a huge yellow rose in front like a headlight, and a dismembered dress form which Bonnie felt would puzzle even the cleverest heathen.

"We're going to rake the yard and burn all the leaves today," Bonnie decided as she and Tommy and Cora Jane hurried home from school on a day when Mama was busy sewing at the church.

Bonnie was a little ashamed to be burning leaves in November, when snow might soon be flying, but she had been busy not only picking Mr. Pippett's grapes but also helping Mama make jelly out of their own late grapes, which grew behind the winery. They had hated to use their precious sugar when they might not be able to buy any more very soon, but next summer Mama could sell the jelly to the summer people at a good profit.

"One thing," said Bonnie, looking at the bare trees and breathing the nippy air, "we won't have to rake but once!" She hurried a little faster. "Oh, I do love a nice bonfire!"

She could almost smell leaves burning already as she came closer to home. Imagination was certainly a wonderful thing. She sniffed again.

"Hey!" yelled Tommy. "What's going on here?"

Fire was sweeping up through the dry grass and weeds of the Bishops' garden. Fanned by a wind from the lake, it was creeping closer and closer to the barn and the house.

"Fire!" yelled Tommy. "Fire!"

Cleopatra, Mr. Pippett's cow, was staring with interest from her pasture.

"Mr. Pippett!" yelled Bonnie at the top of her lungs. "Mr. Pippett! Help!"

Cleopatra galloped toward Mr. Pippett's barn.

"Moo-oo!" bellowed Cleopatra. "Moo-oo! Moo-oo! Moo-oo!"

Discovery

CHAPTER SEVEN

FOR A MINUTE Bonnie just stood there, too bewildered to know what to do next. In Boston when things caught fire, somebody called the fire department, which came clattering down the street with the horses' hoofs beating on the cobblestones and smoke pouring from the funnel of the steam fire engine. But here—

"If I got some brooms and shovels we could try to beat it out," said Tommy. "I read about it in a book once."

"In the woodshed," said Bonnie. "Get that old broom and a couple of shovels," she called back over her shoulder as she ran toward the fire. "Cora Jane, you start pumping water into all the buckets you can find. We'll need water for any sparks that might come flying around."

Coughing from the smoke, Bonnie beat at the burning weeds with her broom. The trouble was that as soon as she had one creeping flame subdued three others advanced ahead of her, jumping from weed to weed stalk in the wind.

Over by Hinchley's, she could see Tommy beating angrily at the fire and sometimes dumping a shovelful of dirt on a particularly stubborn flame. Cora Jane came running from the house.

"There aren't any more buckets," she said. "Oh, dear, I wish Mama would come home."

"Get the dishpan and all the cooking pots," Bonnie ordered, "and tell me when you have them filled."

Bonnie looked worriedly at the old shingles on the roof of the house. They were dry from age as well as a long run of dry weather, and any sparks that lighted on them would likely send the whole roof up like a skyrocket. Where in the world was Mr. Pippett? He could hardly have missed hearing Cleopatra if he were at home, but suppose he wasn't?

Bonnie ran at a finger of fire which was creeping steadily toward the barn. Almost she wished she had been nicer to Homer Hinchley so he would come and help put out the fire—not that she would dream of asking him.

She dug a smudgy fist into her smarting eyes. She was sure that the wind was rising, for the fire was rushing ahead in spite of all the beating and shoveling which she and Tommy could do.

"Faster!" she called to Tommy. "We'll have to work faster!"

Tommy hunched his shoulders and slapped his shovel down harder than ever.

"All right, Albert. You're elected to take care of this." Bonnie turned to see Mr. Pippett sliding a plow off the stoneboat which Albert and Almira were dragging. He unhitched Albert and rehitched him to the plow. "A couple of good wide furrows ahead of that fire and we'll have it stopped."

With his eyes rolling uneasily at sight of the fire, Albert

pulled the plow all the way across the Bishop place from Mr. Pippett's pasture to Homer Hinchley's old barbed-wire fence.

"Once more, just to be sure."

The children, panting and red-eyed, watched Mr. Pippett and Albert thankfully as the plow turned the soil over in a second wide swath.

"I knew Cleopatra would get word to him," said Bonnie.

Cora Jane came running again from the house.

"I finished pumping," she said. "What must I do now?"

Bonnie hugged her little sister.

"Nothing, now Mr. Pippett has come. Oh, my, I believe I could drink every drop of that water myself."

The children watched while the fire crept up to the plowed strip, hesitated, and gradually burned itself out. A few sparks blew over the furrow, but Tommy pounced on them and beat them out before they could really catch. Mr. Pippett halted Albert beside the barn.

"Whew! Now how did that get started?" he wondered.

"What's going on here?" Homer Hinchley came tearing out of his own barn and up to the fence. "Don't you know it's dangerous to start brush fires this time of year? Liable to set folks's houses on fire."

"We didn't start it," cried Bonnie indignantly.

"Be interesting to know who did." Mr. Pippett walked slowly along the fence. "Seems funny it didn't creep over on your side any."

"Wind's kind of southerly," said Hinchley quickly. "Don't get a wind like that every day. Real unusual."

Mr. Pippett had arrived at the spot near Hinchley's fence where the fire had started.

"Seems you'd have come over and helped put it out," he remarked mildly. "I don't doubt these children would have given you a hand if things had been the other way around."

"They might and they might not," growled Hinchley. "How would I know the place was on fire, anyhow? I've been busy in the barn fixing my traps. Muskrat season starts tomorrow, and I'm no more'n half ready."

Mr. Pippett sniffed the air.

"I smell kerosene," he said.

"Must have spilled some on my clothes cleaning up those traps," said Hinchley. "Seems they get rusty, no matter what."

"Didn't smell it on you. Smelled it right around here where the fire started." Mr. Pippett stared off into space. "Never had any firebugs on the island. Have an idea it'd go hard with one if he ever got caught."

"Firebugs!" Hinchley scoffed. "Just spontaneous combustion, that's all it was. Things catch fire just naturally."

"Catch a lot easier with kerosene," said Mr. Pippett. "I expect if anything like that happened again there'd be a lot of inquiring around about who did it, and mostly the truth comes out sooner or later."

"Gotta get back to them traps," said Hinchley. "Can't stand around gabbing all day."

He shambled back toward the barn. Cora Jane slid her hand into Bonnie's.

"Aren't we going to have our bonfire?" she asked in a disappointed voice.

Bonnie felt she had had enough fires to last her for a while, but now she was surer than ever that the leaves in the front yard had better be raked and burned before another day passed. She thanked Mr. Pippett profusely for his help, raided Mama's precious cube sugar for a treat for Albert and Almira, and feverishly began raking leaves into a huge bonfire for Tommy to burn.

"What on earth have you been doing?" Mama exclaimed when she came home a few minutes later. "I never saw such dirty children."

Bonnie giggled.

"Raking leaves," she said with a warning look for Tommy and Cora Jane. "It's very dirty work, raking leaves."

Actually Bonnie did not feel as cheerful as she acted. She did wish she had second sight so she could figure out what Homer Hinchley would do next. He would probably not try to burn them out again, with Mr. Pippett's suspicious warning in his ears, but Bonnie felt sure he would think of some other deviltry. Her shoulders sagged in discouragement. Why did Hinchley want the Bishops out of there so badly? If she knew the answer to that, she might be able to guess his next move but try as she might she could not think of any possible reason for his hostility.

Pop would have known why Hinchley acted the way he did, but of course Pop had lived on Fair Island a long time—long enough to know a lot about everybody there. Bonnie felt sorry for herself for just a minute until she remembered that Pop, in China, must feel twice as puzzled and confused as Bonnie did here on the island.

"At least," she remarked to Tommy, "I don't have to argue with Hinchley in Chinese."

"Huh?"

"Never mind. Just talking to myself." Bonnie quickly changed the subject. "You know, we ought to be thinking about Christmas. Six weeks isn't a bit too much time to get ready."

"You ought to be thinking about supper." Mama stood shivering on the porch with her hands wrapped in her apron. "Aren't you about through?"

Bonnie pushed the last little pile of leaves into the bonfire which Tommy was tending.

"Just about. Mama, where's your sweater? You'll freeze standing there."

"Well, it—it's in there. I—I—"

Gesturing vaguely, Mama went back inside.

"Now what was the matter with her?" Bonnie wondered. "All I asked her was where her sweater was."

Bonnie always liked to see Mama wearing the sweater, which was a soft blue that just matched her eyes. It had taken Mama most of last winter in Boston to knit it, sitting by the geranium-filled window where she could see the sleighs passing in the snowy street. Bonnie gave a little gulp. After all this time, it was silly to feel homesick. Maybe it was just because thinking of Boston made her think of Pop, too, tramping up the street with his sea chest on his shoulder and grinning as Tommy and Cora Jane and Bonnie ran down the walk to fling themselves at him with shrieks of joy.

When Bonnie was little she had always thought that there were two Christmases every year, one at the usual time and one when Pop came home from the sea. This was not only because of the presents which he brought out of his sea chest but also because the Bishops were a family, whole and secure, when Pop was there. It was going to be hard to make Christmas very cheerful this year, the first one since Pop had been gone, but Bonnie was going to try because that was the way Pop would have wanted it.

"Live while you're living," he used to tell Bonnie. "The future's a fine thing but don't miss any happiness while you're waiting for it to come."

That meant that the Bishops must try to forget their worries and keep Christmas the best they could. And the best they could was not going to be anything extra, with almost nothing in Mama's pocketbook.

"We can't spend a cent on Cora Jane and Tommy," Bonnie remarked to Mama one afternoon after school. "We'll just have to make something, though I don't know out of what. Oh, dear, I wish Cora Jane could have a new doll."

Mama was bundling something blue away in her sewing basket.

"I have my presents all planned," she said serenely, "and if you want to give Cora Jane a doll I can show you how to make one. I always liked rag dolls when I was a little girl, and I know we could make a pretty one. There's yellow yarn for her hair and all kinds of leftover material for dresses and coats."

While Mama went to the attic to rummage for scraps, Bonnie peered into the big sewing basket. Four fat blue balls of yarn were hidden there under some of Tommy's undarned socks. For an anxious moment, Bonnie's thoughts flew to the tax money hidden under her best hat. But of course Mama would never dream of touching the tax money for anything in the world, not even for food.

Two steel knitting needles were sticking out of one of the balls of yarn, and the yarn, although it had been tightly wound, had a rather kinky look to it. Suddenly Bonnie remembered Mama shivering on the porch before supper. She put the yarn carefully back where she had found it. There was no doubt at all that Mama had unraveled her blue sweater to knit Christmas presents for her children— maybe mittens with a cablestitch worked up the back or stocking caps with tassels.

Bonnie was very quiet while she and Mama worked on the rag doll that evening. If she thought hard enough, she would surely be able to manage a really nice Christmas present for Mama.

As soon as the breakfast dishes were done the next morning, Bonnie hurried down to the general store, which was crowded with people doing their Saturday shopping. The floor quivered as Mr. Creedle, the storekeeper, lumbered from counter to counter, weighing lard, tying up sacks of brown sugar, making change, cutting off lengths of gingham, and shouldering hundred-pound sacks of flour for women anxious to begin their Christmas baking. On the island, Pop had often explained, six weeks was barely enough time for baking the oceans of Christmas cookies which must be put away in stoneware crocks ready for the perpetual visiting which went on all during the holidays.

"Something for you, Bonnie?"

Mr. Creedle mopped his face with a large red bandanna and looked anxiously toward his wife, who was trying to measure out citron and raisins and match a spool of thread at the same time.

"Looks to me as though you need some help," said Bonnie. "How about hiring me for today?"

"I don't think we could hardly afford any help," said Mr. Creedle.

"I'd take it out in trade," said Bonnie hopefully.

"Well—" At that very moment Mrs. Creedle tipped over a jug of molasses which she had just drawn from the barrel in the corner. "Great day! Never rains but it pours! You're hired!" Mr. Creedle tossed Bonnie a store apron.

"Clean up that molasses first thing before somebody walks in it, then you can weigh out some navy beans from that barrel over there—two pounds to a sack—and tie 'em up with string. And then—"

All day long, Bonnie scurried through the store, fetching and carrying for Mr. and Mrs. Creedle and waiting on such customers as she could. Waiting on customers meant finding what they wanted and writing down the price. At that point, Mr. Creedle must take over. Somebody had passed a counterfeit ten-dollar bill in his store two years before, and ever since he had all but put a microscope on every piece of money before reluctantly putting it into the till.

Mr. Pippett came in with a dozen eggs to trade for some kerosene, and Bonnie sent word home by him that she might not be back before suppertime. Her noon lunch was a handful of crackers and a wedge of sharp orange cheese, which she ate sitting beside the potbellied stove.

"Time to settle up," said Mr. Creedle when it was growing dusk and most of the customers had gone home to cook their suppers. "What was it you had in mind to take in trade?"

Bonnie pointed to some skeins of blue yarn.

"How many of those could I have for today's work?"

Mr. Creedle's hand hovered over the yarn. He put one skein into Bonnie's hand, hesitated a moment, and then added another.

"You did fine," he said. "Guess it's worth that much to have some of the load off us."

"Could I work some more next Saturday?" Bonnie begged. "I think I'm going to need about eleven skeins."

"Stop by and we'll see. Some days we're busy and some we're not—never know ahead of time. Tell you what, if you want to charge the rest of that yarn I guess it'd be all right. Bishops have always been good pay."

Bonnie's eyes shone. It would be wonderful to have Mama's Christmas present safe in the drawer at home. Pop, though, always said, "If you can't pay for it when you buy it, you can't afford it." Regretfully Bonnie shook her head.

"Thank you, but I guess I'd better pay for it as I go along. You don't think somebody else might buy it, do you?"

"Can't tell. I'd be willing to sort of push it under the rest of the yarn, if you want, so nobody'd be apt to notice it especially."

"Thank you. I'd appreciate that."

Bonnie walked home with her precious two skeins of yarn tucked under her coat, safe from the cold rain which was falling. She hurried through the warm kitchen into her room and hid the yarn in the back of her bottom dresser drawer. Mama looked questioningly at her over the blue bowl in which she was stirring up corn bread for supper.

"It's something extra-special," said Bonnie mysteriously. "A Christmas secret."

Every Saturday until almost Christmas Bonnie went to the store early in the morning. Some days there was work for her and some days not; sometimes just a few hours, sometimes all day. The little pile of yarn grew bigger and bigger—five skeins, six, and finally eight.

On December 20, Mr. Pippett went over to the mainland by boat and paid the taxes for the Bishops, bringing the receipt back to Mama and reporting that he had seen the tax collector mark PAID after the description of the Bishop place on the tax book.

"So now everything's all right, is it?"

He smiled down at Bonnie.

"Oh, yes, sir."

Actually, everything was not all right. Bonnie still needed three more skeins of yarn, and yesterday Mr. Creedle had wished her a merry Christmas and had said that there would be no more work because his wife's sister had come to visit and would help in the store, too.

"I finished the doll's coat today," Mama murmured when Tommy and Cora Jane had gone to bed, "and if you want to hem a little handkerchief to put in the pocket we'll have her all ready."

Bonnie nodded and began setting tiny stitches in the doll handkerchief. She still had the initial to embroider on a handkerchief she was making for Tommy, but likely she could find time for that tomorrow. She did not think a handkerchief was a very exciting present for a boy, but all her ransacking of attic and closet had produced nothing that would be any better.

"When you finish that, would you rub the desk with some of those walnut hulls?" Mama asked. "I want it looking nice for the holidays, and I haven't had a minute to touch it. And put on those old leather gloves before you begin unless you want brown hands for Christmas."

Mama hurried into her bedroom, where Bonnie knew she was working to finish whatever it was she was making out of her unraveled sweater.

Bonnie found some walnuts in the woodshed, pounded off the green hulls with a piece of kindling and began rubbing the desk with the inside of the hulls, now juicy brown with stain. The scratches disappeared so well under the stain treatment that Bonnie took everything in turn out of the drawers and cubbyholes so she could reach every scratch inside or out. She pulled absent-mindedly at the carved ornaments on the front of the desk, although she had long ago given up hope of finding Pop's famous secret drawer. For all she knew, it might have been another desk entirely, although she supposed hardly anybody had more than one desk in a lifetime.

She rubbed the pulpy hull inside the little cubbyholes, pushing it carefully into the corners, but she was thinking more about Christmas dinner than she was about the desk. She did wish she could have bought Mama some cranberries. Cranberry sauce might make their roast chicken taste more like a turkey. Grape jelly would be nice, though, or wild strawberry.

Bonnie jumped. A wooden panel had dropped down

from the back of the cubbyhole she was rubbing, and Bonnie's fingers felt something cool and metallic and something else crisp and rustling. She felt a thrill of excitement, like ice water, running down her back. Was it —could it possibly be Pop's secret drawer, found at last?

Merry Christmas

Bonnie's hand shook as she fumbled in the narrow space. Why did she have to be all butterfingers at such an exciting moment?

She gave a final impatient tug and pulled out her treasure —a folded-up dollar bill and a jackknife with a horn handle and "L.B." engraved in curly letters on the metal name plate. Bonnie gave a little sigh. This must be the very knife which Pop had told her about so often—the one he had won at a speaking contest down at the church when he was twelve years old.

Bonnie reached back inside again to see if she could have missed anything, but the space was empty. She spread out the dollar bill and laid the jackknife beside it. She had wonderful plans for both items—plans which she was sure Pop would approve of.

Now that she was paying attention, she could feel a slight bump at the top of the cubbyhole. She snapped the panel back into place and then tried pressing on the bump, as she must have done accidentally the first time. Down came the panel again, as smoothly as though somebody had been using it every day for all these years. It was not magic, after all, but it was near enough to it to make Bonnie feel that Pop had somehow reached out and helped her from some faraway place.

The next morning was cold and gray, and the children

were still eating their breakfast oatmeal close to the warmth of the kitchen stove when Mr. Pippett knocked on the back door.

"Woke up early and thought I might as well milk Cleopatra myself this morning," he told Tommy. "Brought your milk over, too, seeing I was coming." He closed the door quickly to keep the cold out and handed the milk bucket to Tommy. "Going to snow before night," he predicted cheerfully, "which is all we need to make it a real Christmas. Speaking of which, I want to ask you folks to do me a little favor." He laid a huge package on the kitchen table. "Killed this turkey a-purpose for Christmas, and now it seems there won't be but me to eat Christmas dinner. I thought I'd fix a chicken for myself and see if you folks'd take this turkey off my hands. It does hurt me to see good food spoiled for lack of somebody to eat it."

"We'll be happy to take the turkey if you'll come and help us eat it." Mama was saying exactly what Bonnie had hoped she would. "It—it wouldn't be right not to have a man in the house for Christmas."

"Delighted, I'm sure." Mr. Pippett's blue eyes shone with pleasure. "I've eaten many a Christmas dinner in this house with Eben Bishop, and I'll be bound this one will be the best of the lot. I'll be here right at noontime, if that suits."

The snow began to fall just as Bonnie, having managed to escape from Cora Jane and Tommy, started for the store with Pop's dollar tucked carefully into her faded old mitten. The flakes fell in whirling confusion so that she felt as though she were walking through a magic world of white. The muskrat houses out in the marsh looked like miniature igloos, and even Homer Hinchley's slouching figure hurrying to tend his trap line seemed harmless and almost picturesque in its enveloping curtain of snow.

Bonnie could never manage to feel very enthusiastic about trapping, even though Mr. Pippett had explained that it was a way of making part of a living for about half the people on Fair Island. He had taken Bonnie and Tommy down to his own marsh and had showed them how he placed his traps along the trolls or underwater paths where the muskrats swam like miniature submarines to their houses. Bonnie had even seen a few of the pelts drying "fur side inside, skin side outside" on wooden stretchers in Mr. Pippett's woodshed, which was filled with the disagreeable odor of musk.

She thought it would be much more pleasant for everybody if muskrat fur could just be sheared off like wool from sheep, leaving the muskrats to roam the marshes and come back the next year to be sheared again. Pop, she knew, would have chuckled at her idea of a flock of muskrats and would have said gently, "Nothing's quite perfect. Bad things come with the good most times, and there's no help for it."

Bonnie trudged on through the snow to the little white shack which housed the postoffice. A holly wreath hung on the front door, and a wave of heat from the fat stove welcomed Bonnie inside. She did not really expect any letters, but after finding the secret drawer so unexpectedly she was convinced that miracles did happen now and then. The boat company might have had some word about Pop, or Pop himself might possibly have written from somewhere.

"Real Christmas weather at last!" The postmistress smiled cheerfully at Bonnie. "I've got a parcel for you—came in yesterday's mail."

Bonnie stretched out her hand for the package.

"Chicago? Oh, it's from Linda." Bonnie had already sent Linda a box of Mama's very nicest Christmas cookies, decorated with colored frosting and tied up in red tissue paper with a sprig of evergreen tucked into the bow. "Oh, dear, and I can't open it until tonight when we have our tree." The contents of the box slid tantalizingly back and forth as Bonnie tilted it. "You can't tell a thing that way."

"Tonight'll soon come. Anyway, it always has." The postmistress looked at Bonnie over her glasses. "Seems you favor your Pop some across the eyes. Well, a merry Christmas to you!"

Bonnie hurried happily on toward the general store. It was nice to have somebody wish her a merry Christmas and tell her that she looked like Pop, although Pop would have laughed and said, "Well, a misfortune for both of us!"—not meaning a word of it.

Everybody seemed to be in a day-before-Christmas mood. Mr. Creedle, from whom Bonnie bought the last three skeins of blue yarn and a red hair ribbon for Cora Jane, threw in three candy canes for the Christmas tree and a little nosegay of holly and mistletoe for Bonnie's coat. The minister's wife beckoned to Bonnie from the parsonage and sent her home with a shoe box full of green-frosted cupcakes made from a new recipe.

A chickadee flew down from a spruce tree beside the road and chirped something cheerful that Bonnie thought sounded very much like "Merry Christmas." Bonnie scuffed on toward home. As far as she was concerned, Christmas had already begun, and nothing—not worries nor sadness nor Homer Hinchley—was going to spoil it.

Nothing did—not from the moment when Mama gathered the children in the parlor to light the Christmas Eve candles on the tree until the next evening when Mr. Pippett, full of Christmas turkey, left for home across the snowy pasture, with two rosy apples in his pocket as presents for Albert and Almira.

Bonnie slipped away to the twilight quietness of her room to count over in her mind every detail of the Bishops' first Christmas on Fair Island. The smell of cedar and pumpkin pies. Mama's tears and her special kiss for Bonnie at sight of the blue yarn for her new sweater. Tommy's hands turning Pop's jackknife over and over. Cora Jane hugging her golden-haired doll in her arms. Linda's package, open at last and spilling out a dress length of rosy taffeta. The children's gifts from Mama—mittens and caps so handsome that nobody would ever dream that they had once been her old sweater. The secret drawer, triumphantly displayed for everyone's amazement. The turkey, crackling brown on the outside and juicy-tender on the inside. The carols around the old organ, with everybody, even Mr. Pippett, joining in. Bonnie stared contentedly at the snow, blue-white in the moonlight. It had been a wonderful Christmas, better than she had imagined it could possibly be with Pop away.

"Bonnie!" Tommy came rushing into her room. "Where have you been? I've had something to tell you all day, and I never could get a word in edgewise. It's very flustrating."

"Frustrating," said Bonnie. "Well, here I am. You can tell me now."

"Somebody took the flashlight!" Tommy announced. "It was gone this morning when I went down to look."

"Good!" Bonnie was glad that Tommy's frequent visits to the wine cellar to keep track of the flashlight had at last been rewarded. "Now we can start trying to find out who has it." She did not think there was much chance of success, but it would do no harm to try. "I suppose there weren't any footprints in the snow?"

Tommy shook his head.

"Whoever it was must have magicked his way out of there, same as the last time."

"Or else it was still snowing when he left, and it covered up his tracks," said Bonnie.

"I like magic better," Tommy insisted. "The only thing was that the floor looked different."

"The floor? How could the floor look different?"

"Well, it did. It hadn't been swept, because the dust and dirt were still there. The dirt just seemed to be in different places, sort of. You could see the cracks where they laid the stone slabs for the floor. Anyway, you could over on the lake side."

"We'll keep watch." Bonnie thought the business of the floor's looking different was mostly Tommy's imagination. "We'll start knocking at everybody's door and saying, 'Do you have a flashlight? I just swallowed a penny and I want to see if I can find it.'"

Tommy laughed. "Or we could say, 'We want to look under your porch. We lost our pet lion.'"

Tommy went off to bed, calling out unusual ways of borrowing flashlights, and Bonnie sat a little while longer at her window. It had begun to snow again, fat whirling flakes that blotted out the moon and the view of the winery. In a few days now, Mr. Pippett had said, the lake would freeze hard enough for the fishermen to set up their shanties along the shore and fish through the ice as they had done for as many years as he could remember.

The snow was deep but the sun was shining when Bonnie woke up in the morning. Robbie came in meowing indignantly and shaking the snow from his wet paws. Bonnie swept snow off the well platform and laughed at sight of the pump, which was wearing a white cap like a puffy chef's hat.

"Snow's a foot and a half deep and drifting." Tommy came floundering in from milking at Mr. Pippett's. "Some places you can't even find the road except by the fence posts." He blew on his hands to warm them. "Mr. Pippett says we can all ride along when he goes out plowing snow pretty soon."

Mr. Pippett drove up an hour later standing on the platform of his snowplow, which was made of two thick planks set on edge and nailed into a point, then floored with cross-planks. This platform, Mr. Pippett explained, gave the driver a place to stand and to put rocks to weight the plow down as it moved through the deep snow. Bonnie, Tommy and Cora Jane, bundled to the ears, climbed aboard.

"I'll plow your place out as far as the barn—down to the winery, even, if you want me to," said Mr. Pippett.

"Not the winery, please," said Bonnie. "We don't want the snow mussed up because we're watching for footprints. And I guess you better not plow any of the rest, either."

She hated to come right out and tell Mr. Pippett that the Bishops could not afford to pay him for plowing out their place, but she guessed she would have to do it.

"No charge for you, naturally," said Mr. Pippett. "You can work it out by riding along for ballast. I'd rather have people than rocks any time."

"But riding along's just pure fun."

"Fun for some, work for others. Well, if it's a deal, we'll be off. We'll do yours when we get back, in case it snows some more. Albert, we might go to Hinchley's first, if that's agreeable to you and Almira."

Albert and Almira looked at each other, seemed to come to a decision, and plodded past Hinchley's without turning in. Mr. Pippett grinned at the children.

" 'Twasn't agreeable. Always did say they were smart horses. Hinchley hardly ever has his plowed out anyway— hates having people around, for some reason. Well, let's try down the road a piece."

The snow sprayed out along the sides of the plow like showers of diamonds and stacked itself into walls of white beside the road. The children balanced themselves on the plow, red-cheeked and laughing. At the second place past Hinchley's a woman pulled back the lace curtains in the front room and beckoned Mr. Pippett to turn in.

"They sort of expect me whenever it snows," he said proudly. "She wants it plowed out all the way back to the barn, Albert."

After the plowing was done, the woman invited the children inside to thaw out. Bonnie stood beside the kitchen stove, holding out her hands to warm them. Something clattered to the floor, and Bonnie stooped down.

"I wonder if I could borrow your flashlight," she said politely. "I dropped something under the stove."

"My husband lost our flashlight out in the lake last summer," said their hostess. "Let me fetch you a candle instead."

Bonnie knelt solemnly with the candle and fumbled under the stove.

"Got it," she said, dropping a spool of thread into her pocket, "and thank you very much."

Bonnie had a chance to drop the spool in only two other places the whole morning long. At one house the woman brought out a flashlight that was twice as big as the one in the wine cellar, and at the other place a little boy crawled under the table and found the spool by lighting a match. Mostly, they didn't go inside, since Mr. Pippett was anxious to be on his way.

"We could keep this up forever and never find that flashlight," Bonnie grumbled in Tommy's ear as they headed down toward the store.

Mr. Creedle was standing anxiously in the doorway, looking at the drifts, through which a few passers-by were floundering on their way.

"Plow out all the way around, same as usual?" Mr. Pippett yelled.

Mr. Creedle nodded.

"Got a couple of fur buyers in here that can't stir out of the place until the roads're plowed out."

"They're plowed out up our way," said Mr. Pippett, "and they will be down the other end of the island as fast as I can get there."

Bonnie knew that the county paid Mr. Pippett for plowing out the roads, besides what he got from individual owners who wanted their lanes kept clear of snow.

"Early for fur buyers, isn't it?" asked Mr. Pippett when he had plowed an open space all around the store and had pulled up in front for his money. "Especially with Hinchley buying up all the pelts he can get around here."

"Hinchley says he's specializing in Canadian furs this year," said Mr. Creedle. "What for, I don't know, unless maybe somebody'll sell 'em to him for half price. These boys buy from him some, too, when they can get a good enough price."

"They better keep their eyes open if they're dealing with Hinchley," Mr. Pippett muttered to the children. "He's always trying to get first-class prices for second-class furs. And those buyers ought to head back for the mainland today if they don't want to push their boat on the ice a good part of the way. Going to get colder—a whole lot colder."

Mr. Pippett's prediction started to come true before the children even got home. A bitter wind began to whistle out of the north and to whirl the snow in powdery clouds across the fields. Bonnie huddled beside Cora Jane on the plow, trying to tuck her nose into the collar of her coat. She was glad when Mr. Pippett finally finished plowing out around the Bishop place, refused the offer of a cold turkey sandwich from Mama, and started up the road for home, waving his mittened hand at the children.

"We could go down and look at the winery if you want to," Tommy whispered to Bonnie as Mama urged Cora Jane into the warm kitchen and began to shuck her out of her black buttoned leggings. "Mama, we'll be right back."

"Might as well freeze good and stiff while we're about it." Bonnie hurried along the plowed-out path to the barn and then set off through the drifts, kicking up snow as though she were a miniature snowplow herself. "Brrr! It'll be cold in that winery, with the wind howling through all those windows."

The wind had blown the snow through the doorway and window openings into little drifts all the way across the big upstairs room, but downstairs in the cellars it was warmer than Bonnie had expected.

"And no wind down here to cut through to your bones." Bonnie pushed her new knit cap back from her forehead a little. "Now let's see this floor."

Bonnie did not think that the floor looked much different than it always had, except— She motioned to Tommy to come closer with the lantern, which he had picked up in the barn on the way past.

"Well, I guess it isn't anything, after all."

For a moment it had looked as though somebody had been clawing through the dirt just where one slab of stone met the next, but then Bonnie remembered the rats which probably lived down here and the rabbits which perhaps came to visit. How surprised they must have been to have started to dig and then to strike the hard stone floor! Paws digging in dirt would make almost the same marks as fingers, and why would anyone but a rabbit want to dig in the little layer of dirt which had settled on the cellar floor?

"Let's go back to the house." Bonnie shivered a little. "I want to stick my feet in the oven and thaw them out. I never was so cold in all my life."

She was so anxious to reach the comfort of the house that she almost did not stop when she saw the footprints which came over from Hinchley's, looped through the Bishops' marsh, and then returned to Hinchley's, trailing along near the edge of the water.

"Hinchley again! Now what was he doing in our marsh?" Bonnie hopped in Hinchley's footprints through the brown marsh grass, which rattled drily in the winter wind. "There!" She pointed angrily at a trap set in the water near the entrance to a muskrat house. "Now that takes gall! Trapping right on our property! Tommy, run and get the spade." Bonnie shivered as she stepped into an unexpected puddle of shallow marsh water. "Quick, before I freeze to death!"

With the spade the children managed to spring the trap and yank it and the stake it was chained to out of the icy marsh mud. By following the footprints they found three more traps, all of which they pulled out of the marsh and tossed over Hinchley's fence into the deepest snowdrift they could find.

"And I hope he never finds them until spring! That'll teach him to trap in other people's marsh." Bonnie's teeth were chattering, and she was sure her feet were going to freeze solid before she could get to the house. "H-he's n-nothing b-but a g-greedy old p-p-p-poacher!"

Cash in Hand

CHAPTER NINE

HINCHLEY WAS HERE." Cora Jane rushed out to meet Bonnie and Tommy as they hurried up from the marsh. "He was talking to Mama a long time in the parlor."

Bonnie and Tommy exchanged alarmed glances. It was hard enough for Bonnie to get the best of Hinchley, and she was afraid that Mama, with her gentle ways, would be no match for him, especially if he was cross about something, which he usually was.

"He wanted us to reconsider renting him the winery." Mama came into the kitchen and began to roll out a piecrust. "I told him we wouldn't, though goodness knows we could use the money."

Bonnie, who had stiffened at mention of Hinchley's renting the winery, relaxed again. Mama surprised her sometimes by being as firm as a rock at the most unexpected moments.

"Was he mad?" asked Bonnie.

"He probably was." Mama's tone was airy. "But I was so horribly polite that he couldn't say he was mad even if he was."

Bonnie knew exactly how Mama must have acted—so sweet and helpless that nobody could possibly dream of being horrid to her. It was just another example of catching more flies with honey than with vinegar, and it came perfectly naturally to Mama, who was always eager to please everybody.

"He couldn't stay so very long to argue about it, anyway," said Mama, "because I invited him into the parlor, and the stove wasn't lit in there. Bonnie, why do you think he wants that winery?"

Bonnie shrugged.

"Maybe because he can't get it. Whatever it is, I don't think it's for anything good. Of course, as he says, he may need more space for his furs, though I'd say it would take all the furs in Canada to fill that big barn of his."

"I mistrust him," said Mama mildly.

Bonnie giggled. Pop always said that when Mama mistrusted somebody the worst was sure to happen. Once she had mistrusted the captain on a ship Pop had been on, and it had turned out that the captain had tried to beat Pop out of part of his pay. Another time she had mistrusted the landlady's pet cat, and the very next day the cat had come in and stolen a fish that Mama had on the table all ready to cook for supper.

"Big or little," Pop sometimes said solemnly, "if your mama mistrusts anybody or anything, look out for trouble!"

"It's just a feeling I get," Mama would say vaguely. "Something not quite the way it should be."

Bonnie agreed that Mama was right in mistrusting Hinchley, especially since Bonnie had found those traps in the marsh. Every day she expected to hear Hinchley's harsh voice accusing her and Tommy of stealing his traps, although of course it would ill become a poacher to threaten the owners of the land he poached on.

"And anyway the traps are lying right there on his own property," she told Tommy, "just waiting for the spring thaw."

Any kind of a thaw seemed very far away to Bonnie, for it grew colder and colder all through January, with more and more snow on the fields and more and more icicles lengthening on the edge of the kitchen roof. A little colony of fishing shanties sprang up on the thick ice all around the island, and the children went fishing a few times with Mr. Pippett, although Mama was always uneasy about them, declaring that the ice might thaw unexpectedly or that the children might fall into the holes cut through the ice under the shanties for the fishing lines.

Some years, Mr. Pippett said, there was considerable money to be made by selling fish to a man who came out from the mainland to buy for the hotels in Cleveland and Toledo. This year, though, the man did not come, and Homer Hinchley took one load of fish over to the mainland on his bobsled, returning with much less money than anybody had expected. After that, most people caught fish only when they or their neighbors needed some to eat. Bonnie, who had had dreams of earning some extra money toward the June taxes by selling fish, gave up and spent her spare time helping Mama, who was making a quilt out of the scraps from her sewing.

"Somebody might want to buy it next summer," said Mama cheerfully, "and if not we'll have a new quilt for ourselves and it won't cost us anything but our work and what thread it takes."

Mama was really only killing time with the quilt, waiting until the material for Clarissa Creedle's wedding dress came over from the mainland. Mr. Creedle had sent clear to Chicago for it—ivory satin with imported lace for the trimming—and Mama expected to be busy at least two weeks setting in the lace medallions and fixing the drape of the skirt just right. Clarissa wanted Mama to begin sewing on it the minute the material came, although Bonnie could not see what the rush was, since the wedding was not going to be until the ice was all out of the lake, probably the middle of March.

"What does ice in the lake have to do with it?" Bonnie asked Mr. Pippett.

"Nobody'll come from the mainland unless the lake is frozen good and solid or else not frozen at all," Mr. Pippett explained. "Nobody wants to get stuck halfway between here and there."

"I guess that's reasonable."

Naturally the Creedles would want everybody possible to come to the wedding, since they had written all around that Clarissa's dress was going to be an exact copy of a gown in one of the Paris fashion magazines. Bonnie had expected Mama to be dreadfully nervous at even the thought of trying to copy such a creation, but Mama was apparently looking forward to it. She had, in fact, grown much less timid now that everybody on the island thought of her whenever they needed dresses for really important occasions. The trouble was that there were not nearly enough important occasions, especially in the dead of winter, to keep her busy.

"If you didn't have to go to school and put out fires and help your mother and chase poachers, I could likely get you a job, if you were a big strong man instead of a girl," Mr. Pippett told Bonnie one day. "I hear—and I know you won't go telling this all around the island—that Mr. Lewis is none too well satisfied with Homer Hinchley for a caretaker. Seeing Hinchley's house is right next to the Lewises' it ought to work fine, but it doesn't. Homer doesn't attend to things—always seems to have his mind elsewhere, besides being so surly to man and beast."

"How about you doing it?" asked Bonnie.

"Can't even get through my own work—fruit trees and the hauling business and all—much less take on any extra for Mr. Lewis. Could if I was twenty years younger—maybe."

Bonnie went inside to find Hinchley sitting in the kitchen trying again to persuade Mama to rent the winery.

"I'd pay you good rent," he said, obviously trying to twist his features into a pleasant expression. "More'n it's worth, really."

"Why?" asked Bonnie curiously. "Why would you pay more than it's worth?"

Hinchley's face turned red, and Bonnie thought he was going to jump up and walk out, but he stood his ground.

"Because it's just what I need," he muttered. "Handy and plenty of room and—"

"I'm sorry to refuse you again," said Mama gently, "but I don't think my husband would like me to rent it."

"I know he wouldn't," said Bonnie stubbornly.

"Just like throwing money in the lake, turning down a good offer like that. 'Tisn't as though anybody else'd rent it," Hinchley called back as he walked down the path. "You think it over, Mrs. Bishop, and I'll drop by some other day."

"Some other day when I'm not here to back you up." Bonnie smiled at Mama and reached down to pet Robbie, whose purring affection increased as the smell of baking fish spread through the kitchen. "I wonder how much he actually would pay for it. He certainly is determined to get it."

Hinchley came sauntering by the next Monday when Mama and Bonnie were hanging up the wash, which froze solid as soon as the icy wind hit it. Bonnie was pretty sure he had planned to ask Mama again about the winery, but, seeing Bonnie, he only remarked sourly, "Kids're supposed to be in school. Truant officer'll be after you."

"Not after me, he won't," said Bonnie airily. "The teacher in my room didn't come today."

Hinchley scowled and strode off down the road.

"I'm going in and start on Cora Jane's jumper," said

Mama. "I ripped up that old wool dress in the attic, and I think I can get just enough pieces out, if I figure around a little."

Bonnie finished emptying the wash water in a snowdrift and went out to the barn to feed the chickens. She had an even dozen now—Anastasia and her children, who had grown up to be as big as their mother. There were two eggs in nests in the hay, and Bonnie put one in each coat pocket. As cold as the weather was, she was surprised that the hens bothered to lay any eggs at all.

It did not seem that it could stay this cold much longer, when spring was supposed to be here in just six weeks. The first day of spring was one date Bonnie could never forget, because it was also her birthday—March 21. Pop had carefully explained to her that on that date, which was the vernal equinox, the sun was crossing the equator coming north and day and night were exactly the same length.

"So it's quite a day, even besides being your birthday," he used to say. " 'Tisn't every little girl who brings spring right with her."

Pop had not always been home for her birthday, but whether he was or not Bonnie knew that he wore a flower in his buttonhole in honor of the occasion. At home it was always a faded old paper rose, since flowers were never in bloom in Boston by March 21. But when Pop was in some foreign port, he often had a real flower—lotus, frangipani, wild orchid—according to where he was. Bonnie loved to hear him name them over, each one making her think of distant lands that were as strange to her as they were familiar to Pop.

Dreaming of sweet scents and flowery Oriental gardens, Bonnie walked straight into the line of frozen washing and was slapped in the face by a dancing pair of Tommy's overalls—which was what came of not paying attention. Holding her smarting cheek, she hurried inside and put the two eggs in a blue bowl in the pantry. She could hear Mama's sewing machine humming in a corner of the dining room like a bee in an acre of clover.

It seemed odd to be at home alone with Mama, with no Tommy or Cora Jane to fill the house with their talk and their questions. It was a cozy sort of feeling, though. Maybe, since the younger children were not here, Mama might let Bonnie have a grown-up cup of tea with her instead of the watered-down variety, mostly milk and sugar, which the children usually drank. It was too bad that tea was not more nourishing, seeing Pop had brought home so much of it at various times—green, black, orange pekoe, jasmine, and a few others with Chinese names which Bonnie could never remember. She always loved to open the little lacquered canisters with their delicate painted sprays of flowers and to sniff the faint dry aroma of the tea leaves inside.

Suddenly the hum of the sewing machine was interrupted by a crash, a thud, and a sound like metal being torn apart.

"Bonnie!" cried Mama. "Bonnie! Come here!"

"Mama, what is it?"

Mama pointed with a quivering finger at the sewing-machine head, which now had a jagged break across its middle.

"I was sewing along the same as usual, and it fell apart, just like that," wailed Mama. "Oh, dear, and Mr. Creedle expects that material for the wedding dress any day now."

Bonnie stood and stared, overcome by the catastrophe. Unless the sewing machine could be fixed—and it looked completely wrecked to Bonnie—Mama would not be able to sew anything, not Clarissa Creedle's wedding dress nor any of the things people would want made all summer. And unless Mama sewed they could never in the world pay the taxes. And if they did not pay the taxes—Bonnie shuddered.

"I'll run right down to the store," she said. "Mr. Creedle sells sewing machines, so he ought to know something about fixing them."

She left Mama looking mournfully at the wreckage of her machine and ran at top speed for the store until she swallowed so much cold air that she had to slow down. Mr. Creedle spied her at the door.

"Material just came in the mail," he said jovially. "It's beautiful."

"Just beautiful," chorused Mrs. Creedle. "Clarissa's going to look perfectly lovely."

"Our sewing machine!" Bonnie gasped. "Could you come and see? Something awful's the matter with it."

Mr. Creedle clapped his hand to his head.

"Oh, never! Don't tell me that!" He rushed around the store, snatching his coat from the counter, his heavy cap from the cracker barrel, and his wool gloves from under the cat, who was sleeping cozily on them in the sunny window. He gave his wife a wild look. "Manage however you can, my dear! I'll be back when I get here!"

Mr. Creedle set off at a fast clip, turning so red in the face that Bonnie finally said, "No need to kill ourselves getting there. It isn't going to get any more broken than it already is."

Mr. Creedle subsided to a slow trot and was puffing only slightly when he burst into the Bishop house and knelt in front of the broken machine, over which Mama was still wringing her hands. Mr. Creedle made dismal sounds in his throat and shook his head slowly from side to side.

" 'Tisn't anything minor," he declared. "Might be it could be welded, but that'd mean a trip over to the mainland, and the man over there's slower than molasses in January getting anything done. It's liable to be a month, and Clarissa and Mrs. Creedle want that dress started this week at the very latest."

He gazed in silent thought at the broken machine.

"I don't have a machine in stock right now, either. I'd have to send to Cleveland for one and that'd take time, too—across the ice, and it's liable to break up one of these days. No, that won't do."

143

"We couldn't afford to buy a new one, anyway," said Mama timidly.

Mr. Creedle seemed not to hear her.

"There's that one I sold to Cousin Genevieve Creedle a couple of years back. She's got no more use for a sewing machine than I've got for a ruffled parasol. She never finished paying for it, either." He put his cap back on his head and tucked his ears into large red ear muffs. "I'll get it from her and have it here first thing tomorrow morning so you can start on that dress. I'll make you a rock-bottom price, too—forty dollars and your old machine."

"Forty dollars! But, Mr. Creedle, we don't have any money," said Bonnie.

Mr. Creedle beamed at Bonnie and Mama.

"Things are never as bad as they seem, now, are they? I knew I could think of something."

He bounced out of the house, and Mama and Bonnie looked questioningly at each other.

"You don't suppose—" Mama began.

"I don't suppose anything," said Bonnie. "He just couldn't hear us with those ear muffs on." She sat down in the little rocker and held her head. "Forty dollars! It might as well be four hundred or four thousand or— Oh!"

She wished she could be perfectly sure what Pop would do right now. He sometimes used to say, "Desperate situations require desperate remedies," and Bonnie was sure that this was a desperate situation. Could any situation, in fact, be more desperate than not being able to earn a living?

"We'll have to do it," Bonnie decided, "but we'll need to figure it just right to get the whole forty dollars all at once. Now, Mama, see what you think of this."

A few minutes later, Bonnie looked out to make sure that Hinchley's barn door was open, a positive sign that he was working with his furs. Then she hurriedly put on her coat and hood and went noisily out of the house, slamming the door and calling loudly to Mama, "I may go and visit the minister's wife awhile. She promised I could copy off her cupcake recipe for you."

Bonnie rounded the bend in the road, waited a minute, and then came hurrying back. Just as she had expected, Hinchley's fresh footprints in the snow led over to the Bishops' kitchen door. He must not have waited until she was even quite out of sight to start pestering Mama again about renting the winery. Bonnie did not particularly relish being the kind of person that even a man like Hinchley avoided, but right now there was no help for it. She let herself quietly in through the front door and tiptoed into the dining room, where she could hear every word that was being said in the kitchen.

"Well, I suppose I might reconsider," Mama was saying in a hesitant voice. "As you say, we don't actually use the winery for anything, though I don't think my husband—"

"I always figured you were a sensible woman, when you're left to yourself," Hinchley interrupted. "Now then, you know as well as I do that that old ruin isn't worth much. I figure ten dollars a month is a good rent for it."

"Let's just forget it then," said Mama. "I had some suitable figure like twenty-five in mind. I guess I'd be making a mistake to rent it at any price."

"You've got mighty big ideas!" yelped Hinchley. "Twenty-five dollars a month for a building that's a hundred years old if it's a day? Why, it's liable to fall down on me. I'll give you fifteen."

Bonnie hoped that Mama was wearing a suitably reluctant expression.

"Bonnie has always been against my renting it, anyway," Mama stepped to the window. "Why, I do believe she's coming back already."

"How about twenty?" Bonnie could tell from Hinchley's voice that he wanted to close the deal before Bonnie arrived to put up any further arguments. "Starting today."

"Two months in advance, please," said Mama. "My husband always said—"

Hinchley made a spluttering noise.

"I'll make you out a check," he said wearily. "I don't know why they say men are hard dealers. Women have them beat all hollow."

"Cash," said Mama. "Checks are too much trouble, with the bank on the mainland and us over here. Oh, hello, Bonnie."

Bonnie hastily slammed the dining-room door and came into the kitchen.

"What's going on here?" she demanded.

"Well," said Mama, "I—I rented the winery to Mr. Hinchley."

Bonnie tried to look as angry as possible.

"Rented the winery!" she exclaimed. "Why—"

Hinchley, who had been rummaging frantically in his pockets, pulled out three bills from his wallet and a fourth from an inside pocket and laid them in Mama's hand.

"Ten, twenty, thirty, forty," he said rapidly. "You've taken the money; the deal's closed. Busy day. G'by."

He plunged out the door and across the fields toward home.

"It worked!" cried Bonnie jubilantly. "Mama, you ought to be an actress. You were perfectly wonderful!"

Mama picked up the bills and looked at them carefully.

"That's a lot of money," she sighed, "and I don't think any good is going to come of it. I've—I've got a feeling."

The Disappearing Boat

CHAPTER TEN

Hinchley hasn't done a thing down there." Bonnie stood in one of the upstairs windows looking toward the winery with Tommy's spyglass. "And after all that big talk about putting in doors and windows! I don't believe he even goes down there except once in a long while."

Bonnie wanted very much to do some exploring at the winery but Mama kept insisting that the children must stay away unless they had a real errand.

"We rented it to him," said Mama, "so we can't go poking around there, any more than if it were a house."

Bonnie felt that she could easily think of an errand— something she needed to borrow from Hinchley or a message from somebody, if anybody ever sent Hinchley a message, which she doubted. She was giving the matter her best thought when Tommy took the spyglass and looked out into the lake.

"Mail's coming," he yelled. "Let's go watch."

Bonnie hurried into her coat and bundled Cora Jane into hers. Mostly nobody was very much interested in watching the mail, which came by the regular boat in summer and by sled in deep winter when the lake was frozen solid. Now, though, when the lake ice was breaking up in spots, everybody on the island who could spare the time went to the boat dock to watch the metal rowboat with the mail floundering across patches of hard ice, expanses of open water, and the even more uncertain areas of floating ice floes.

"Not quite weather for boating, but not quite weather for sledding, either," said Mr. Pippett, who was down at the dock, too. "There they come—those black specks 'way out there."

Bonnie waited impatiently until Tommy finally handed her the telescope. At once the distant specks became two men pulling the mail boat over the ice floes far out in the lake. As she looked, the men reached the edge of a floe, climbed into the boat, and shoved off into a channel of open water. Bonnie shivered.

"It looks dangerous," she told Mr. Pippett.

Mr. Pippett nodded.

" 'Tis. Floating ice hits the boats sometimes and tips them over. Those men earn their pay twice over. I'd take up some other line of work myself."

"They're hauling the boat up on the next floe." Bonnie handed the spyglass to Tommy. "I guess I don't want to look any more. It's too scary."

The men and the boat drew slowly nearer, buffeted sometimes by the waves and moving precariously over tossing ice floes. Bonnie gave a sigh of relief when they finally reached the dock, around which tip-tilted cakes of floe ice were piled every which way.

There was not much use waiting until the mailbags were brought out from under the lashed-down tarpaulin which had protected them from the icy water. Linda was the only person who would be apt to write, and Bonnie had had a letter from her just the week before. And only the week before that, Mama had had another letter from the World-Wide Steamship Lines, saying that since they had found no trace of Pop he must be considered lost and would be so recorded on the company's books.

The steamship company had also promised Tommy a job whenever he was grown-up, as they did for all the sons of men lost on company business, but a job eight or nine years in the future was no help right now, even if Mama were in any mood to let Tommy go to sea. Besides, Bonnie still was not ready to admit that Pop was gone for good, in spite of all the time which had passed.

"It's a long way from Hong Kong," she frequently told Tommy when she felt the need of reassuring herself. "It'd take anybody a long time to get back."

Secretly, though, she wondered if it would take quite this long. She dreamed sometimes that Pop was struggling through jungles, walking across deserts, or swimming through battering surf while Bonnie reached out to help him and could never reach quite far enough.

Thinking of Pop made her decide to wait until the letters were sorted and until she was sure that there was nothing for the Bishop household. Tommy and Cora Jane were staring, wide-eyed, at the two mail carriers, who were thawing out in front of the postoffice stove.

"Come on!" Bonnie tugged at the children's sleeves as

the postmistress distributed the last of the letters. "Mama will think we're lost."

The day had turned cloudy, and the mud on the road was freezing again into icy ruts.

"It'll be nice when it dries out for good," Bonnie grumbled. "They could leave March out of the calendar for all I care—except for my birthday."

"Yoo-hoo! Bonnie!" The minister's wife was waving her apron from her front door. "Would you do me a favor? Please leave this flashlight for Mr. Hinchley on your way home. He loaned it to my husband to walk home by, that night our buggy tipped over in front of his place."

"Yes, ma'am. We'll see that he gets it."

Bonnie looked excitedly at Tommy as she trotted back out to the road.

"Open it up as soon as we get out of sight," she said. "It certainly looks like the same one." She bent over to see the tiny "B" scratched on the inside of the cap. "Just what I thought! Well, that was easy, after all our fussing. We're just plain lucky."

"I don't see what's so lucky about it," Tommy complained. "It was just old Hinchley snooping around, the same as usual. Why couldn't it have been somebody exciting, like an Indian or a mysterious pirate?"

"Pirates and Indians are sort of scarce any more," said Bonnie. "And I still would love to know why Hinchley would be snooping around a wine cellar in the dead of night and who was with him and especially how they got out of there without coming through the door. Well, we'll certainly return the flashlight to him." She knocked several times on Hinchley's door. "Nobody home. We'll have to go down to the winery to find him. I guess Mama would think that was a real errand, seeing it was the minister's wife that asked us."

Bonnie felt very cheerful as she picked her way down the muddy lane to the winery. Even if it was rented to Hinchley, it made her happy just to step inside again and to think of all the fun she and Linda had had here during the summer afternoons which now seemed so long ago.

The winery hardly looked different at all, except for a few furs hanging from the rafters to dry and a faint odor of musk. The wind must blow most of the smell away, howling through the windows all the time. Bonnie hesitated at the top of the stairs.

"Hey, you!" Hinchley bellowed from halfway down. "You got no call to be snooping around here. I rented this place fair and square, and if I want visitors I'll say so."

Bonnie held out the flashlight.

"We brought this back," she said sweetly. "The minister's wife asked us to return it and to say thank you very much."

"Coulda left it up at the house, couldn't you?" growled Hinchley.

"And maybe have somebody steal it off the front steps?" asked .Bonnie. "Funny thing, that flashlight looks sort of

154

familiar. I wonder if I could have seen it around some-where."

Hinchley shot her a quick look that might have been suspicion or maybe only annoyance.

"I carry it in my hip pocket most times," he said. "Comes handy for dark places. Well, g'by now. Next time come to the house or wait until I get there. I'm not aiming to be pestered with people down here, even if I have to put a padlock on the door."

"You haven't got a door," said Bonnie acidly. "And you're perfectly welcome for the flashlight. Anything for a neighbor."

Hinchley's face reddened but still he did not say "Thank you," and Bonnie could see him standing at the winery door watching even after the children were back in their own house.

Bonnie was cross at Hinchley for being so surly, but she was crosser at herself for forgetting about catching more flies with honey than with vinegar. Her last remark had been practically all vinegar, and she was sure that Linda would not have approved of it. Still, maybe the usual rules did not count with Hinchley—a thought which she knew was only a poor excuse for poor conduct.

"There's a perfectly strange man coming up the front walk," said Mama, peeking through the parlor curtains. "Now what would he want?"

"You'll likely never know unless you let him in." Bonnie did not mean that remark to sound as disagreeable as it did, either. It was just that she did wish sometimes that Mama were not so timid. "Maybe it's somebody that heard about Clarissa Creedle's wedding dress and wants to order one for somebody himself."

Mama smiled. Clarissa's dress was truly beautiful, even handsomer than the picture in the fashion magazine, and Bonnie could hardly wait for the weather to settle a little more so that the wedding could finally take place. Bonnie tugged on the front door, which flew open with unexpected suddenness and catapulted her halfway into the dining room.

"Mrs. Bishop?" The stranger took off his hat politely. "I'm a federal officer. May I speak with you for a minute?"

Mama stood back hesitantly, and the stranger stepped inside.

"Will you come into the parlor?" asked Mama timidly.

The stranger shook his head.

"I'll keep you only a minute." He consulted a small notebook. "I believe that on February sixth you bought a new sewing machine from Mr. Creedle."

"It wasn't new," said Mama in a fluttery voice. "It was secondhand, though just as good as new."

"The details don't matter. What I want to know is where you got the money."

"Wh-what?" Mama stammered. "Why, we—"

"Four ten-dollar bills, I believe. All I want to know is where they came from."

Bonnie gasped. What business was it of anybody where the Bishops got their money as long as they didn't steal it? Bonnie could feel her temper rising in spite of all her efforts to keep calm and collected. Maybe somebody did think they stole it. Maybe that was why this man was snooping around. The stranger glanced at Bonnie's stormy face and held up a soothing hand.

"I don't mean to suggest that you came wrongly by the money. I just want to know where you got it."

"We got it from Homer Hinchley next door," said Mama quietly. "He rented our old winery and paid for two months, cash in advance."

"And that was the money you used for the sewing machine?" The officer closed his notebook and stepped to the door. "Thank you very much. That gives me exactly the information I need."

"But why do you need it?" insisted Bonnie, still ruffled at the questioning.

The stranger merely bowed slightly to Mama, said, "Please do not report my visit to anyone," and strode down the front walk.

"People are pretty curious," Bonnie sputtered, "when they send a policeman around to find out where we get our money."

"Bonnie!" Mama's voice was unexpectedly crisp and firm. "I'm sure the man had some good reason for wanting to know. And it's no credit to your upbringing when you stand and glower at people as though you were going to fly at their throats. You might at least have given the man a chance to explain."

"He never intended to explain," Bonnie muttered under her breath. Then, seeing Mama's troubled look, Bonnie flung her arms around her and cried, "Oh, Mama, I'm sorry!"

She never used to act like this in Boston, all bossy and chip-on-the-shoulderish. Of course in Boston she had never had anything to worry about because Pop, even when he was off on a voyage, always had everything arranged ahead for his family. If Pop did not come back soon to attend to things, Bonnie supposed she would have to go right on being bossy and quarrelsome until she was so set in her ways that she would never be able to change.

Every morning after that, her first thought was to remind herself to be as soft-spoken as Linda, no matter what happened to annoy her. Very little did, since school was always very much the same and since she took pains to stay at a distance from Hinchley, who seemed to be unusually busy all of a sudden. Bonnie saw him starting for the mainland one day with what she supposed must be a load of furs, and another day a fur buyer came to the Bishop house asking for Hinchley and was directed to the winery by Bonnie with a politeness which she felt sure even Linda could not have surpassed.

Feeling very smug, she gave herself two gold stars on the secret chart which she kept hidden in her dresser drawer— one star for politeness and another one for minding her own business. There was a third space on the chart for not being bossy, but so far nothing had come up to keep from being bossy about, so she felt she did not deserve a star for that.

Waking up early on the morning of her birthday, she decided it was probably silly to try to improve her disposition with gold stars, but at least it helped keep her mind on the problem. All the time, though, she knew that whenever Hinchley started to make trouble again, she would be the one who would have to do the fighting, chart or no chart.

"Happy birthday!" Cora Jane stuck her head into Bonnie's room. "Mama says to get up. She's making French toast for breakfast."

Bonnie scooped Robbie out from under the bed and scratched him behind the ears.

"My birthday and Saturday and the first day of spring all rolled into one!" she exclaimed. "It can't help being a wonderful day."

Sniffing from her open window, Bonnie thought she could catch a faint suggestion of spring weather. The wind from the lake did not seem quite so cold, and the fields were showing traces of green. A rather chilly-looking robin was hopping across the yard, looking hopefully for worms. Best of all, the lake, although gray and rough, was clear of ice and already dotted with a few boats. It would not be long now until all the bite would be out of the air and the little new leaves would be uncurling on the trees.

From the kitchen Bonnie could already smell her birthday cake baking in the oven. She must remember to stay out of the way until Mama could frost and decorate the cake, because birthday cakes in the Bishop family were always kept secret until they were borne, ablaze with candles, to the supper table.

It seemed to Bonnie that the hours until suppertime would never pass. In the morning she went down to the store and then to the boat dock to watch a launch leave for the mainland with Homer Hinchley among the passengers. In the afternoon she dusted the parlor and the dining room and straightened her dresser drawers, and still it was not quite four o'clock. Cora Jane was sewing spring clothes for her Christmas doll, Mama was visiting Mrs. Creedle down the road, and Tommy was in his room reading *Adventures among the Cannibals*.

There seemed nothing for Bonnie to do but to sit in her room staring out at the drizzle of rain which was bringing dusk at least an hour earlier than usual. She could hear a boat motor far out in the lake, and she could see a rowboat, too, moving briskly along the shore in the mist. Bonnie rubbed her eyes and looked harder. The boat should be passing the winery now and almost up to Hinchley's, but it was not. It had seemingly disappeared right before her eyes, or else it was coming up on the Bishops' beach. Bonnie jumped to her feet.

"Tommy, I'm going down to the shore. Do you want to come?"

Tommy clattered down the stairs, and Cora Jane came running, too, scattering doll clothes in all directions.

"I don't think Mama would like you out in the rain," Bonnie told her little sister. "You better stay here."

"I don't think she'd like you out in the rain either," Cora Jane argued, but Bonnie closed the door firmly and rushed down the lane with Tommy.

Oddly, there was no boat in sight, even though the children went to the very edge of the water and looked all along the shore and out again into the lake. There was a slowly moving dim shape farther out, but it looked a dozen times as big as the boat Bonnie had seen.

"Must have sunk," said Tommy.

"It couldn't have—not in that little minute. But just in case it did, maybe we ought to go into the winery and see if we can find Mr. Hinchley and tell him." She grinned at Tommy. "One excuse is as good as another, I guess. I saw Hinchley going on the ferry this morning, but how do we know he didn't come back?"

The winery was creepy in the approaching twilight, and Bonnie wished they had a lantern to light their way. Tommy clattered blithely down toward the cellars.

"I hear a noise," he said. "Like somebody rowing a boat."

"I hear something, too." Bonnie pulled Tommy behind an old wine barrel in the dimness of the second cellar. "Only it sounds like people talking now. Maybe we better go back. Oh, look!"

She pointed a quivering finger at the floor on the lake

side. One of the stone slabs was rising, and lantern light shone up around the opening.

"Old buzzard's supposed to come back from the mainland and help us." A burly man stuck his head through the opening and with a grunt slid the slab to one side on the stone floor. "What do we do now—wait?"

Peering fearfully around the wine barrel, Bonnie saw that a boat was drawn up directly under the place where the stone slab had been—a hidden boatwell underneath the winery. The burly man clambered up from the boat, which rocked a little under his feet.

"I want to get gone out of here," he grumbled. "Nighttime's better, so's we can come in through the door Hinchley fixed and not rassle that blasted stone slab around." He gestured toward the door which Tommy had tried so often to open. "Oh, well, toss up them furs. No harm unloading them, even if Hinchley ain't here."

A hoarse laugh came from a stooped-over figure in the boat.

"No harm in the world. We just gotta have him here when we take the you-know-what out of them air chambers. Don't want him saying we held anything out on him."

Bonnie tugged at Tommy's hand and gestured up the stairs. The burly man turned his back and bent again over the boat as his companion tossed a bundle of furs up on the stone floor. Bonnie and Tommy scuttled silently from behind their barrel and up the first few steps. Bonnie dared to breathe a little sigh of relief.

"Whoa, there! What do you think you're doing?"

Her wrist was seized suddenly in a rough grasp. Homer Hinchley was there, blocking the way so that even Tommy could not wriggle through.

"I said stay out of here!" roared Hinchley. "And that's what I meant! Get up those stairs now, and if I ever catch you around here again, I'll have the law on you for breaking and entering. Get, now!"

Bonnie thankfully snatched Tommy's hand and scurried toward the head of the stairs.

"Bonnie," said Tommy breathlessly, "what did that man in the boat mean about the 'you-know-what in the air apartments'?"

"Air compartments, huh?" Hinchley made two leaps and again cut off their escape. "That's a horse of another color." He pulled the children roughly down into the cellar. "You with your big ears and your big mouths! You got yourselves in a peck of trouble this time!"

Birthday Gift

CHAPTER ELEVEN

WE HAVE TO GO HOME now," said Tommy in a shaky voice. "It's Bonnie's birthday, and Mama has the cake all ready."

"We just wanted to tell you about the boat," Bonnie chimed in, "but seeing they're friends of yours—"

Her voice trailed off. She had never been afraid of Hinchley before, but she was now. Her breath failed her and she could only shiver in Hinchley's grasp and stare at him as he stood gnawing his lower lip and muttering under his breath. He fixed the boatmen with a cold eye.

"Blabbermouths!" he exclaimed. "Did you have to tell everything you knew in front of these kids? Here, hold onto 'em."

The burly man twisted Bonnie's arms expertly and painfully behind her.

"How did we know there were any kids snooping around?" he demanded in an injured voice.

"Broke my neck getting this place fixed just right," growled Hinchley, "and now a couple of kids come along and spoil the whole setup. Looks like you can't get Bishops out of your hair, no matter what." He chewed more furiously on his lip. "Unless— Lots of accidents happen to kids, seems as though."

Bonnie looked at Tommy, held firmly by the other man, a small sharp-faced character who reminded Bonnie of a

rat. Tommy's eyes were roaming desperately in all directions as though he expected help to come from the solid
stone of the walls. He turned his head as though listening
and then stared fixedly at Bonnie. She nodded faintly. She
heard it, too, dim and far away—the sound of Cleopatra
bellowing in her pasture.

"Moo-oo-oo! Moo-oo-oo! Moo-oo-oo!"

Bonnie did not take much comfort from the sound, but
she glanced reassuringly at Tommy to keep his spirits up.
Cleopatra was probably bellowing just to hear herself
bellow. Nobody at the Bishop house would be yelling for
Mr. Pippett, because nobody would know that Bonnie
and Tommy needed help. Mama wasn't even home, and—
Suddenly Bonnie felt the tiniest ray of hope. Cora Jane!
Could Cora Jane have followed them down here, not far
enough to be trapped but far enough to know that something was wrong? The hope died. Even if Mr. Pippett did
come, he would never be a match for three husky men,
especially when they were as desperate as these seemed
to be.

"Get the rest of those furs unloaded," Hinchley ordered.
"Then we'll have room in the dinghy to take the kids out
to the cruiser. Won't be anybody looking for them out
there."

Bonnie shuddered. She felt as though she were in the
middle of one of her very worst nightmares, except that
there did not seem to be any way of waking up from this
one.

"We weren't hired for no such business as that," the rat-faced man objected. "No rough stuff, the boss said, just a nice quiet hauling job."

Hinchley turned on him.

"You better get different ideas—and quick," he declared, "unless you want to spend the next ten years in some cell."

"Now look," said Bonnie indignantly. "You don't think we came down here without telling anybody, do you? If we don't come right back, you'll be the first one they'll be after."

"Who'd know I was even down here today? Nobody saw me come."

"If I saw that boat clear from my house, somebody must have seen you coming down here," Bonnie argued, "rain or no rain."

Hinchley ignored her.

"Snap it up with those furs!" he told the boatmen. "We haven't got all day. What if somebody comes looking for these kids?"

Hinchley backed Bonnie and Tommy into a corner and stood menacingly over them as the rat-faced man climbed sullenly down into the dinghy and tossed the last bundles of furs up to his partner. Bonnie thought she heard a muffled sound upstairs, but then she decided that it must be only the wind and the rain.

"What was that?" Hinchley raised a silencing hand. "Quiet, everybody!"

The muffled sound suddenly turned into a crash, followed by the sound of clanking chains.

"Must be that ghost of yours," said Bonnie sarcastically. "Chains and all."

"Ghost, nothing! Just another dirty snooper, most likely, tripping over that pile of traps upstairs. I'll settle his hash!" He started up the steps with his flashlight and a stubby black pistol, which he drew out of his pocket. "Keep the kids back in the corner out of sight, and not a sound out of any of you!"

Bonnie could hear Hinchley's stealthy steps going up the stairs, then silence, then a scuffle, and then Mr. Pippett's voice, loud and angry.

"We'll go down and take a look for the children, just the same," he shouted. "March ahead of me down those stairs, and don't forget this musket's pointing straight at your spine. Besides that, I've got a mighty itchy trigger finger."

The boatmen exchanged looks and ranged themselves silently alongside the stairway. From there, Bonnie saw, it would be easy to reach up and grab Mr. Pippett before he even knew there was anybody down there. From her corner, Bonnie saw Hinchley's feet descending the stairs. Then his legs came into view and then all of him, with his hands high over his head. Then came Mr. Pippett's feet four steps higher, and then—

"Go back!" screamed Bonnie. "They're going to grab you!"

It was too late. The burly man seized Mr. Pippett around the legs and pulled him down the last few steps. The musket rolled on the floor and went off with a loud bang. Hinchley snatched his flashlight from Mr. Pippett and retrieved the black pistol from Mr. Pippett's hip pocket.

"Jumped me!" Hinchley panted. "So now we've got three of 'em instead of only two! Tie him up for now. We'll have to come back for him after we get these kids out to the cruiser." He cackled disagreeably. "No use sinking the dinghy just when we got things rolling again."

Mr. Pippett sat up dazedly as Bonnie and Tommy flung themselves furiously on their captors and were brushed off as casually as though they were no more important than buzzing flies. Bonnie looked pityingly at Mr. Pippett. He had done the best he could for them, and now he was in as bad a fix as they were. Nothing, she felt sure, was going to save them now.

"Let's get going!" As Hinchley pushed Bonnie toward the boatwell, she turned and kicked him sharply on the shins. "Why, you—"

Hinchley's howl of pain was interrupted by a cool voice from the stairway.

"Get over in that corner, and keep your hands up!"

Even in the wavering lantern light Bonnie thought she could recognize the federal officer who had asked Mama about her sewing-machine money. He spoke more sharply as Hinchley and the boatmen stood in their tracks for a startled moment.

"Up with those hands!" the officer repeated. "We've got the place surrounded."

Hinchley made a sudden rush for the boatwell, diving frantically through the hole in the floor, with his two boatmen scrambling after him. Splash! That was Hinchley. Splash! Splash! All three sank from sight as abruptly as though they had jumped off a cliff. Spluttering noises were followed by shouts from outside. The officer went over and looked down into the boatwell.

"I told you you were surrounded," he remarked calmly. "Our men outside towed your boat out of there just a minute ago. All right, boys. Fish 'em out!"

Two more officers came from the stairway, and Hinchley and the boatmen were dragged dripping from the boatwell and lined up against the wall. The chief officer gave Hinchley a chilly glance.

"Now that you've had your swim, we'll get down to business. Is there anything you want to say?"

"You got nothing on me," Hinchley glowered. "Can't a man unload a few furs without—"

Somebody gave a mighty heave on the old lake door, which opened to let in an officer who had evidently been guarding the outside entrance to the boatwell.

"Went all over their cabin cruiser out there as soon as they left for land with the dinghy," he reported. "Canadian registry. Couldn't find a thing. Jones is searching the dinghy now, but there's no trace of the stuff there, either. Any luck here?"

"It's congealed, that's what it is!" Tommy announced importantly. "In the air compartments."

"Concealed," said Bonnie automatically.

"You!" snarled Hinchley, glaring straight at Bonnie. "You're a nosy, bossy trouble-maker! None of this woulda happened if—"

"If you hadn't been doing what you shouldn't," Bonnie retorted in her most vinegary voice. "Just like that time with the pigs."

Hinchley, still muttering angrily, lunged toward Bonnie for a dangerous moment. Someone pushed abruptly through the lake doorway and shoved Hinchley roughly back against the wall.

"What do you think you're doing?" the newcomer yelled. "I'll knock you into the middle of next week and back again. Deviling my children! Using my winery for your skulduggery!"

"Pop!" Bonnie stared unbelievingly at her father and then rushed into his arms. "Oh, Pop!" She looked up into his face, which in just that little minute became again as familiar as when he had gone away. "Oh, I knew all the time you'd come back!"

"Me, too!" said Tommy. "Most days. But other days—"

"I had plenty of those other days myself," said Pop soberly.

Bonnie stood and stared blissfully at her father, hardly noticing what was going on around her.

"I've got it!" The officer who had been searching the

dinghy came in through the lake door with a packet of crisp fresh bills. "Right where the little boy said. Lots of it, too. Good enough to fool almost anybody. Real high-class counterfeit money!"

"Counterfeit money!" gasped Tommy. "Oh, boy!"

"Fur business made a good cover-up, looks as though." Mr. Pippett leaned on his musket and watched wistfully as the officers started to herd their prisoners up the stairs.

Hinchley threw a venomous glance in Bonnie's direction, but Bonnie kept her mouth tight shut. Pop hated bossy, sharp-tongued women, and Bonnie hoped desperately that he had not heard her remarks to Hinchley a few minutes before.

"I wonder if Hinchley's printer friend in Canada went into this deal with him, seeing their cruiser is from Canada," mused Mr. Pippett. "Well, I might as well go home and clean my musket. Looks as though the excitement's over. See you tomorrow, Luther. It's mighty good to know you're safely home."

"Home to stay, too," said Pop.

Bonnie tugged at his hand as they walked through the darkness toward home.

"Pop, how—"

"The officers gave me a ride up from Cleveland on their boat. I used to know one of them years ago, but I never dreamed they were coming right to our old winery."

"But, Pop, please tell us—"

"When your mother and Cora Jane can listen, too," Pop promised.

Cora Jane, rubbing tearful eyes and shivering with excitement, came out of the woodshed and buried her face blindly in Bonnie's coat.

"Mr. Pippett told me to stay right here," she wailed, "until he saw what was going on, and then it got dark and Mama didn't come home."

"You did exactly right," said Bonnie. "You and Cleopatra."

Light flared in the kitchen, and Mama opened the back door.

"Bonnie! Tommy! Cora Jane!" she called. "Come and get washed up for supper. Where on earth— Oh!" She gave a little gasp and burst into tears on Pop's shoulder. "Luther! Oh, Luther, is it really you?"

Cora Jane cried, too, and so did Bonnie, and even Tommy wiped away a few tears while pretending to get something out of his eye. Pop surveyed his weeping family.

"Always was damp weather on the island," he remarked, "but I never saw it rain tears before."

"Pop," begged Bonnie, "please—"

Pop sank into a rocker beside the stove.

"All right," he said. "I'll begin, before Bonnie dies of curiosity. What happened was that Chinese bandits got me when I went for a little walk outside of Hong Kong. Then it took weeks and weeks to convince them that it was a case of mistaken identity—that I wasn't some rich American with plenty of ransom money back home."

A broken ankle, a penniless walk back to Hong Kong from the bandits' stronghold, a roundabout voyage home —Bonnie's mind was much too busy for her to listen to more than the general details. She was already planning how Pop could get Hinchley's job from Mr. Lewis and how the captain on the summer boat to the mainland would likely give him some work and how he could trap muskrats in the marsh and raise vegetables in the back pasture.

Bonnie opened her mouth and then shut it so fast that she bit her tongue. She had remembered just in time that Pop was in charge of the Bishop family now and that the old bossy Bonnie, with all her troubles, could disappear for keeps. No more quarreling with Hinchley, no more fussing about the tax money, no more worrying about pigs in the garden or poachers in the marsh. Bonnie gave a sigh of contentment as Mama set her birthday cake, twinkling with lights, in the middle of the table.

"And I couldn't even buy you a present," said Pop ruefully. "This certainly didn't turn out to be much of a birthday for you."

Bonnie snipped a bright red geranium from one of Mama's house plants and stuck it at a jaunty angle in Pop's buttonhole.

"Not much of a birthday?" she exclaimed. "It's the very best birthday I ever had—and the biggest present!"